Ian Wedde was born in 1946. He is the author of six novels, fourteen collections of poetry, two collections of essays, and a monograph on the artist Bill Culbert, as well as edited anthologies and art catalogues. His fiction has been praised for the vigour of its language and the wide scope of its ideas. His first novel, *Dick Seddon's Great Dive*, was awarded a National Book Award for fiction in 1976 and was briefly notorious when a sex scene in it was discussed in the House of Representatives. In 1986, *Symmes Hole* established him as a major voice in Pacific fiction; the novel was hailed in the *Listener* as 'a remarkable and even triumphant achievement'. More recently, his satirical novel of 100% pure tourism, *The Viewing Platform*, came out in 2006, and the futurist dystopia *Chinese Opera* in 2008.

Ian Wedde is the recipient of numerous awards, fellowships and grants. Among the more recent are the Meridian Energy Katherine Mansfield Memorial Fellowship at Menton in France (2005), a Fulbright New Zealand Travel Award to the USA (2006), an Arts Foundation Laureate Award (2006), and a Distinguished Alumni Award from the University of Auckland (2007). He was awarded an ONZM in 2010. He lives and works in Auckland.

The Catastrophe

IAN WEDDE

Victoria University Press

VICTORIA UNIVERSITY PRESS
Victoria University of Wellington
PO Box 600 Wellington
victoria.ac.nz/vup

First published 2011

National Library of New Zealand Cataloguing-in-Publication Data

Wedde, Ian.
The catastrophe / Ian Wedde.
ISBN 978-0-86473-647-5 (pbk.)
I. Title.
NZ823.2—dc 22

Published with the assistance of a grant from

Printed by Printlink, Wellington

This book is dedicated to the poet Mahmoud Darwish and the people who taste his words in their speech.

CHAPTER 1

The taxi, clean and white with a bright blue light on top, did a careful U-turn and stopped on the far side of the rain-slick street. A passenger stepped out into spilled light behind the taxi on the footpath side. The woman was wearing a black, trousered suit. She opened a small red umbrella and stood there as if thinking what to do next. Then she strode forward. It seemed strange that the taxi had parked on the other side of the street from the woman's destination. Her determined strides made the direction of her intentions clear, but she seemed to be avoiding eye contact with the first-floor window of the restaurant where he sat with his glass of wine and, pushed to one side of his plate, the remains of a Provençal braised rabbit and some bits of unsatisfactory salt pork. Sure enough, under the partial cover of the umbrella, her head flicked quickly up at his window.

But not 'his' window, after all, since she didn't know he was sitting next to it – since, in fact, she didn't know him. Nor did he know her. But she'd deliberately made the taxi stop over there, after it had first parked in front of the restaurant. Her hesitation was also, somehow, determined. The woman seemed to be thinking her way through the approach she would make. Or perhaps she was thinking ahead about the direction in which she would prefer to leave, since the white taxi waited while she paused again on the footpath below the restaurant, closing the red umbrella.

She was in her 50s, he guessed – a tall, gangling woman whose bony frame he extrapolated from her striding gait and the long, oddly pale fingers with which she gripped the strap of a shoulder bag. Black and shiny, the bag was slung against her hip. Its purpose wasn't clear – it could have been business-like or an expensive accessory. The details of her appearance, even her movements, weren't easy to see clearly through the rain-streaked window. Obvious features, like her hands, were exaggerated. They seemed pale and prominent – maybe she was wearing gloves of some kind? The rest was vague. Yet the direction of her intentions seemed clear.

She wasn't all that interesting. But what else was there to look at? He was bored. He'd been bored ever since Miss Pepper. His 'food is love' mantra going iffy around him, like left-overs forgotten in the back of a fridge.

He arranged the bits of fatty pork in a triangle shape.

Bored *and* alone. The only solo diner in the wretched place. Though hardly lively, it was at least half full of neighbourhood regulars taking the easy *plat du jour* option on a miserable night – with the possible exception of a dodgy older-man-young-woman unit in a discreet booth. He'd even begun to look forward to the lanky woman entering the restaurant when she'd first stepped off the far curb and crossed the road the way she did, so determined. The taxi remained where it was. Perhaps she was making a delivery? She had silvery hair that swung a hand's-width below her ears. He saw it when she jerked her umbrella aside to help her balance on the slick street. She took another quick look up at the restaurant windows. She was wearing elegant, wedge-heeled boots. Her straight hair was grey, though it could have been very blonde, given the darkness outside and the irregular shafts and patches of light that entered the street from the bars, their street-front windows and entranceways, coloured neons, the yellowish street-lamps. Then she paused, furling her umbrella, and disappeared under the restaurant awning below his window. He waited hopefully for her to appear over by the maître d's desk.

Meanwhile he refilled his own glass and dabbed up a little of the rabbit's winey gravy with a piece of bread. The pastimes of the lonely traveller. No, not lonely. Alone. The alone traveller's time-passing observations. While he allowed his critical faculties slowly to assemble detailed thoughts about his meal – beyond the fact that it was rubbish.

Because he'd lowered his face over the plate to get the moist bread to his mouth he missed the woman's arrival. What he saw first as he lifted his face to follow the bread with a sip of wine was the very big man in the booth at the opposite end of the room from the maître d's desk. He'd stood up with his pale linen jacket hoisted above his broad hips and was pushing the table away from himself against the other side of his booth, pushing it against the young dark woman in a black, sequined top who was also struggling to stand up. The man's huge face seemed to be stretched around the entire front of his bald head by a feral grin of fear.

The gunshot came from the direction of the reception desk. The big man flinched as if stung. The tall woman from the taxi had dropped her luxurious bag on the floor next to the desk and now she began to cross the room with long strides, the revolver held out in front of her in both hands – which he saw did have pale gloves on them. When she fired again it was the young woman who flew sideways and crashed out of sight behind the table, dragging the tablecloth and everything that was on it with her. Then, at the third shot, the big man seemed to jump in the air before sitting down almost comfortably on the banquette behind him. He was clutching his thick neck. It looked as though he might have spilled the *Tomates aux crevettes* down his chin and chest. That was that.

The lanky woman swung the revolver in an arc and the maître d' put his hands above his head. Other diners had started to scream and shout but the woman, whose hair was indeed grey, said nothing. She left her expensive-looking bag where it was and stepped sideways to the door of the restaurant. She seemed to be making decisions according to a scrupulous, cautious logic. Her pauses were thoughtful, her subsequent movements decisive. Slow, slow, then fast – like a dance step. She moved decisively through the door leaving her strategic hesitation behind her in the arrested poses of the diners, the waiters, the maître d' with his hands above his head and the sleeves of his dark jacket pulled back towards his elbows. A ridiculous amount of black hair sprouted from the cuffs of his white shirt.

The *plat du jour* diners were frozen in their seats, so he was able to get to the exit quickly. He saw the maître d' make an imploring gesture at him, but he couldn't hear what the man was saying over the sound of the yelling in the room. The shape of the man's imploring words was 'No! No!', but could as well have been 'Go! Go!' No one blocked his way out the door, not even he himself, though one of his own voices was shouting 'No!' in his head while the other insisted, 'Go!' The 'No!' voice was expecting to get shot on the other side of the door, but the 'Go!' one was certain the grey-haired woman would have gone down the restaurant stairs at full speed towards the taxi parked across the road. He had the taste of winey sauce, bay, thyme, juniper and rabbit in his mouth, together with the cleansing sip of nice plain Rousillon Coulet Rouge. Like a greedy gulp, he flew heedlessly down the stairs.

Ever since Mary Pepper he'd hoped – believed, even – that the small signs of his ageing were funny if nothing else. The little fart that broke from him in a hotel elevator as he bent to pick up his suitcase; his refusal to 'act his age'. But lately it had become clear that his preference for young company and his refusal to accept his physical limitations were embarrassing to most people. Not least his ex-wife. His Miss Pepper.

His 'Thé Glacé' – his TG. He was getting more and more fussy and pedantic, she'd said with affectionate resignation, before things got nastier. That was when her Mary Pepper–wealthy Chelsea voice started putting phrases like 'get real' in quotation marks. As if she was quoting herself. Which she was. Who'd have thought it? Not long ago, 'gusto' was his middle name.

And yet his professional reputation had increased for the very reasons his youthfulness had lost credibility. Now he wasn't a maverick any more. The professional insincerity of restaurant staff told him this. He was wise in judgment and foolish in self-knowledge. This was why he dined alone these days, like a widower, having lost the companion known in his syndicated columns by the soubriquet Thé Glacé; why he travelled like the bon vivant roué he wasn't, really.

The street-side door of the white taxi was unlocked and he opened it and fell across the woman in the back seat as the cab accelerated away from the curb. The unlikely word 'providence' had flashed on in his mind like the 'Taxi' sign on the taxi's roof. Why was that? Nana Gobbo had often muttered the word during his childhood. Or the Italian – *provvidenza*. Then, he didn't know what it meant – and it still filled him with dread and excitement.

'Really stupid,' said the woman. She hadn't even screamed. He couldn't place her accent. It was French but something harsher as well. It made the 't' spitty and turned the 'u' into an angry grunt. Her gun pressed into his ribs where huge breaths were stopping his speech. What would he say, when he could? The woman was clearly cursing as she adjusted her clothing efficiently with one gloved hand while the other kept the barrel of the revolver pressed into the side of his chest. The driver wasn't a cab-driver, that was clear. Sweat was running down the back of his thick, furry neck. He too was cursing in a foreign language that forcefully conveyed rage. The windscreen wipers seemed to be conducting his rant as they swept squalls of rain aside. The white taxi sped out of the narrow street of bar-fronts and neons and entered a broad boulevard lined with palms. The constriction in his chest opened as well – his breath began to flow steadily, like the orderly lanes of traffic.

'You forgot your bag,' he panted. A little, rabbity burp came up with the words. He held the shiny thing with both hands against his heaving chest.

'And the umbrella, I suppose?' The woman's laugh was metallic – a clashing sound high in her bony chest. 'God almighty,' she said with a guttural rasp of emphasis on 'mighty', and dug the gun into his ribs. 'Are you a madman?'

The driver yelled something in the language that sounded furious whatever he was saying. He smashed one open hand against the dashboard of the car and yelled again.

'Cross turds with turds, you'll get shit,' translated the woman. 'That's what he thinks. What do you think?' She prodded him. 'Sit up better, please – further over there.' Her English was confident but odd. She arranged herself firmly in her seat, getting her clothes straight and covering the revolver with a turquoise silk scarf.

What did he think? He was amazed. He was in the car. He was here, now. He'd run out of the restaurant and across the road, he'd jumped into the car. He felt as though he'd left himself behind – as though he'd jumped out of time. He didn't even know how he'd done it. Now he was in the taxi with this angry driver and the woman who'd just shot two people in the restaurant he was meant to be reviewing. A tremendous fluttering began to interfere with the breathing he'd only just recovered.

'What,' demanded the woman, 'so now you're going to be sick?'

'I don't know what I think,' he gasped, his pride a little wounded. 'What I was thinking,' he corrected. 'Why I did this.' The fluttering began to go away. 'But I knew I was going to, the moment I saw you cross the road to the restaurant.' This was barely true and only after the fact, and the woman scoffed as if she saw this.

'What do you do? Not a police – a journalist, perhaps? You think this is an opportunity?' She paused, and then laughed her chesty, metallic bark of a laugh again. 'A *scoop*, as you say?' She made a derisive scooping gesture with her free hand.

'I'm a food writer,' he said. 'I write about restaurants and food. I travel around and do this. It can get very boring.'

Now the woman's attention sharpened with obvious scorn. She turned her scoop into an incredulous summary of the car's interior. 'And what do you think this is – *un amusement*?' She spoke the French word crisply but then relayed something to the driver in the other language, what sounded like a joke or an insult; the language also sounded angry when she spoke it. The driver smacked his dashboard again and yelled something.

'He has for you a suggestion about food,' the woman said. Suddenly she looked tired. Her heavy beige eyelids drooped. 'You wouldn't like to hear it.' The gloves she was still wearing were like those synthetic ones some line cooks wore these days, and they transformed her derisive gestures into a kind of mime. The artificial looking, nail-less hand not covered by the scarf was very pale; it accentuated her olive complexion.

She picked up the large shiny bag that he'd rushed down the stairs with. Now, in the intermittent light of street lamps that also gave the woman's face a filmic appearance, he could see that it was one of the ubiquitous fake luxury-brand items that black North African men sold on the beaches of the Ligurian coast where he'd written memorably about *Cappon Magro*, the Genoese Christmas Eve speciality. She held the fake Gucci bag out to him with her free hand, the other holding on to the pistol under her scarf on the seat between them.

'Please to put this bag over your head, Monsieur Gastronomique.' She pushed the bag against his chest. 'Over your head. This bag that you . . .' Then she was impatient – she slapped the bag hard against his face. 'Over your head, now!'

'You want me to . . . ?' But he knew what she wanted. He put his head inside the bag and slumped against the cheap vinyl cladding of the seat. The inside of the bag smelled of . . . it smelled of the bales of such bags that black peddlers hauled off and on the trains along that coast of bug-eyed, spiny fish. It was brand new. Maybe it had only ever held the gun. A glossy, coloured, travel magazine-type illustration of the oily *Cappon*'s pyramidal shape came to his mind, with skewers of prawns, anchovies and mushrooms splendidly adorning its crown. He'd written about it with 'gusto'. A 'food is love' moment. The image was briefly vivid inside the bag.

'He said, you should try eating your own shit.' The vinyl seat cover on her side squealed as she shifted across to yank the bag further down over his head. Then her bony hand found the cellphone in his breast pocket. When chilly air blew into the back of the car he guessed she'd chucked it out the window. The secret of *Cappon Magro* was in the quality of the air-dried fish and keeping the artichokes separate from the other cooking vegetables. The woman's voice was slightly muffled and he could smell his own gamey breath inside the bag.

'My friend has a limited vocabulary, mostly about shit,' said the woman. 'But on the other hand, you. A *food writer*.' That metallic bark. Then a word in the angry language. The fluttering in his chest had stopped. How strange it was to feel almost peaceful under the circumstances. He sat with his head inside the soothing darkness of the bag, which smelled new and luxurious, not fake. An image of the excessive pile of Genovese fish and vegetables, with its odd adornment of prawns, anchovies and mushrooms on skewers and its moat of greenish *salsa verde*, flicked on and off in the darkness which was also a kind of darkness in his mind. Thé Glacé, skinny wee Mary Pepper, had always liked these rich, *proletarian* dishes, and others such as the Bedouin *mansaf,* though how she'd fitted them in was a miracle. Their rationale seemed to be to include as many ingredients as possible at the same time, a kind of gluttonous economy – though TG baulked at the *mansaf*'s crowning glory of a boiled sheep's head. Nonetheless, despite the head, gusto was what they'd had in common, at the beginning.

Out there in the white taxi, the bony, olive-skinned woman with long hands clad in pale synthetic gloves, and the driver whose thick neck had been running with sweat, continued to argue in the language that was angry even without their apparent rage. They seemed to be providing a furious commentary on the gleaming *Cappon Magro* in his mind which, now, had begun to alternate with the *mansaf* and its glutinous skull.

The impatient shriek of a zip announced the woman's desire to get out of the car. Her door opened and slammed, propelling a gust of cool air into the back seat. A stink of diesel and culvert sludge came into his bag. Where were they? Nowhere salubrious. Then the driver, he guessed by the curses, opened the door on his side and yanked him out by the arm. The building they were in smelled like an oily, exhaust-fumey garage at first. Then they went through another door into somewhere domestic – there was a homely smell of burned or badly cooked food – and he was pushed up some narrow, creaking stairs. He counted two flights. Then he was thrust down into an armchair. He tried to be compliant, even helpful, but when he reached up, panting, to take the bag off his head, someone smacked his hand away. He felt chilly air on his stomach where his shirt was untucked. He could hear the sound of dense, fast-moving traffic in the distance. Then someone closed some shutters and fastened a window and the traffic noise receded. A door closed. Did that mean there was no one in the room, or that someone was waiting silently in it? He needed to pee. He was very thirsty. It was stifling inside the bag.

'So,' said the woman's voice. 'You just sit there? With the bag? It's okay? You are comfortable? You don't want to take it off? So obedient, it's very good.'

'I need water. I want to use a toilet,' he said. It felt as though he was complaining to himself.

'What, in the bag?' The woman's chesty laugh moved closer. She slowly lifted the bag from his head. '*Voilà tout*!' she exclaimed. 'Now I am a magician.'

He took deep breaths. It was as though he'd woken up – everything was vividly present. Certainly, it was scorched chickpeas and garlic that the room smelled of. And cigarettes. Its bare plastered walls were brightly lit. There were two dirty green armchairs in a cluster with his own, a low glass-topped table in the centre, an ashtray filled with filter-tipped cigarette butts, an empty Coca Cola bottle, two used espresso cups. He was facing a closed window with greenish wooden jalousie shutters outside the glass. A brown water stain ran from the sill to the wooden floor. So this was an old building – not concrete, at any rate. The woman was standing behind him. He didn't turn his head. He didn't dare to. He guessed she could see his thighs trembling, but he couldn't stop them. Maybe he was going to throw up after all.

'Please,' she said. 'May I have your personal document? You have it?'

'The toilet,' he said. 'I need the toilet. The lavatory.'

When the bag came back down over his head he cried out and his body, for the first time admitting that he was afraid, betrayed him by emitting a little jet of pee. Then the woman's hand in his armpit urged him to stand and hurried him forward. The bad cooking smell was stronger outside the room, and he could hear the harsh, argumentative voices of two men downstairs. Then the woman pushed him into the stink of a dirty toilet and a door slammed behind him. He yanked the bag off his head. There was a squat hole in the tiled floor, a hose with a rusty shower-rose hanging on the wall, a silvered mirror, a small grubby hand-basin, a dirty towel.

His hands were shaking. He peed towards the lavatory hole as best he could, then suddenly bellowed loudly and vomited a geyser of rabbit and wine across the floor. That made him feel braver as well as better – even defiant. He washed his hands and face under the tap and stood there dripping. No way would he touch that towel. He wouldn't put the bag back on his own head, and not just because it had been on the filthy floor. Then he opened the door.

The woman was waiting across the landing under a yellowish light, a look of haughty disgust on her face. Her hand was dismissing a man coming rapidly up the stairs – a thick-set older man, not the angry driver, with a full grey moustache and a balding head. The man shrugged indifferently and turned back down the stairs. The woman was holding open the door of the room with the armchairs in it. He walked past her and sat down.

'So you can see,' said the woman, leaning against the wall by the window, 'that we have now a problem. That you have made for us a problem. What is your name?' She was ignoring the fact that he'd been sick, or else she didn't care. He didn't care, either. He felt as though he'd been moved forward by another decision, one he didn't even know he'd made until he was in the situation it had created. Until he'd become one of the decision's consequences. He was someone else. He'd jumped out of his past. Or he'd sicked it up.

'You don't need to know my name,' he said. 'I'm sorry. I was stupid. I was bored. You can just let me go. I won't tell anyone.'

The woman lifted an eyebrow. Then she suddenly smacked

the flat of her hand against the wall behind her, making him jump. 'But you have seen everything. You think I am stupid also?'

'I saw what everybody saw.'

'But then you get in the taxi. And maybe everybody see that.'

'It was a mistake.'

'A mistake for you, a problem for me.' The woman took a long stride and sat on the arm of the chair opposite him. She held out her hand. 'Your document. You have it perhaps in your jacket.'

Close up, in the hard light of the room, he could see that her face was hatched with fine lines which, however, made her skin look papery thin and delicate. There were dark bags under her big, protuberant eyes, and her cheeks were pocked with large pores or the remnants of some disease. Yet she was as striking close-up as she'd been when he'd first seen her across the road from the restaurant, glimpsed in tricky patches of light, moving quickly from shadow to shadow. Could that be why he'd run down the stairs and jumped into the taxi – his 'mistake'? Was this his 'problem'?

'You think this is funny?' She snapped her fingers. 'Your document, please. Passport, something like that.' Her mouth smiled but her eyes didn't – the fragile skin at their corners remained uncrinkled. Yes, as usual, his snigger had been inappropriate. 'You are famous perhaps. Mr Free Lunch.' To him her joke was both surprising and offensive, but she enjoyed it. Her eyes crinkled a little at last and she barked her curt, chesty laugh.

What difference did it make? The price of his foolishness could already have been a bullet. He could have had his head pushed into the foul lavatory. They could have thrown him out of the car once his head was in the bag.

'My name is Christopher Hare. Hare I am. A terrific name for a food critic you might think.' She didn't get either joke –

she pinched at one of the bags under her eyes as if to relieve some pressure there, and kept her other hand extended. Anyway, they'd always been lame jokes. He didn't need TG to tell him that, though of course she had. He took his wallet out of his jacket pocket and extracted the passport from it. 'I sometimes use a pen-name, do you know what that is? A pen name? *Nom de plume*?' The woman flapped her extended hand impatiently. 'A false name. So most people don't know who I am. Including me.' He tried another joke: 'Or where.' Still she didn't smile – her eyes, attentive but moody, watched him steadily. 'The people at the restaurant – they don't know who I am.' He handed her the passport. 'Or they don't care.' She opened the passport and glanced up at him from its photograph; she made a droll 'Tut' sound at the comparison. 'If their terrible hare's anything to go by.' *Shut up,* he told himself. Then he took a deep breath. That fluttering again. 'So why did you do it?'

Why did you do it? He pressed one hand against his panting chest – of course he was asking himself the question as well. He half expected her to answer it for him.

She was turning the pages of his passport with decisive flicks of her fingers, tilting it on its side to look at visas. She lifted her head and stared at him. Again, she seemed tired, or even bored.

'That man, he had also a false name. He had many false names. He was false, as you say. But we found him.' The smile that wasn't a smile. 'As you saw for yourself.' She handed the passport back to him. 'And why? Because it was necessary. But also to show that hiding is not possible.'

She stood up and he tried to do so also, but she stopped him with an abrupt gesture, one arm thrust out, her palm held up, big fingers splayed.

'You are maybe quite famous, Mr Hare, or whatever you prefer. Your false name as you say. A famous food writer. You have a wife? A good cook? Maybe she wonders if you run away with a beautiful woman like me.' She coughed, or laughed. 'What we have to do I think is make this problem into a useful thing. That is always what I like to do. Your mistake, yes? Your stupidity. We cook it.'

She crossed the room with that decisive speed, as if she'd rehearsed the move. By the time he got to the door it was locked. He was about to raise his fist and bang on it, and shout – kick it. But then he remembered the moment when he'd stood up in the restaurant and run out after the woman who'd just shot two people. How he'd flown down the stairs. How could he possibly have done that? How? This was something he had done. No one had done it to him. He had done it. He, Christopher Hare. *Christopher Where*, as TG had begun to say a while back. *Where are you Christopher? Christopher Where?* What was the point of making a fuss? He must have wanted this to happen. This was the moment he'd wanted to be in. No, impossible. But yes.

He opened the window and then the wooden jalousie. The chilly air was smelly but felt fresh, like an old-fashioned sorbet between courses. He sucked it in through the bilious taste in his mouth. The window faced old apartment buildings across a dark, nondescript street. Between the buildings across the street he recognised the profile of hills behind the city, pricked with lights. So he was facing inland, perhaps from somewhere down towards the docks. There was a smell of drains, maybe the harbour. He'd run down the restaurant stairs – could he climb out the window?

He pulled the shutters back together and fastened the glass behind them, shutting himself in. He felt himself moved forward by another decision, another one he hadn't really made by himself. He was reflected there in the window, a dim phantom, thickset, his dark shirt hanging out under his jacket, his hair a mess, his full-moonish face tinged with pallid light reflected from the green jalousie slats. He seemed to be pouting. That was what everyone always said he did.

'*Malade de jalousie*,' he said, exaggerating his out-of-focus pout, watching himself do it, remembering the French phrase. 'Christopher Where.' When he said his joke name aloud he knew exactly where he was – he was Hare, now! – and at the same time he knew he was completely lost.

CHAPTER 2

Food is love.

There it was, out of the blue, the email via her website message board, taunting her. Their secret code. And in the subject line, 'From your husband Christopher.' Her *what*? How many months had it been? And who the hell was this cunt Maya Yazbeck whose email address he'd used? What kind of catastrophe had the silly fool got himself into now?

Food is love! Christopher, you dolt.

Oh for God's sake. Did she need to be reminded of what drove her crazy about him?

'You know what drives me crazy about you? You horrid man?'

My God – where to start?

Straight away, the nostalgia bit. She'd put on Joe Jackson. The songs made her flat less empty.

Is she really going out with him?
Is she really going to take him home tonight?

Christopher's curly hair that always needed a trim, his shirt always hanging out. The way he either tipped too much, or forgot to. His suitcase that pinged open and spilled unwashed stuff on the way to a late check-in. The way his mouth was rather rose-buddy and he seemed to be smooching his food sometimes, not eating it.

She'd adored that, and the little kisses he popped into the space between her chin and collar bones, as though the part of her he loved best was where she swallowed. Little moist popping kisses that made her shiver while goose-bumps appeared all over her.

He called it her 'chicky skin'.

Sometimes he made it happen by walking his fingers up her bare arm, across the back of her neck, and up on to the top of her head.

'The Southern Alps,' he would murmur. 'Arthur's Pass – lucky old Arthur.'

So corny; she was old enough to know better. But she couldn't help it, the bumps rose up and then his lips descended on them, pop pop pop. They rose up all over again, more than ever. But it wasn't true that he loved her throat best. He loved all of her. That nibbly rosebud mouth – '*Chris*topher!'

Joe:

'Cause if my eyes don't deceive me
There's something going wrong around here

For God's sake – the songs were already ten years old when she *met* Christopher, but they still pushed all her weepy buttons now.

She loved the way he mostly didn't eat very much at all. How he tasted things with an expression on his face like a child at a party, serious and thrilled at the same time. Then, sometimes, he'd say 'Yum!' and bolt a plateful. *Such* a greedy-guts. Then ask for more, but not eat it. He'd build a Dogon cliff village with his polenta while the waiter glared. He liked talking and playing games while they ate.

He played with his food. He talked with his mouth full. His manners were shocking. He was funny. He utterly charmed people, even when he was rude. He didn't care.

*

On that first epic trip together he was always asking her what she thought. Was he interested, or just having fun? Towards the end of that trip, the squalid little Venetian place.

'Do you like it? Really? On a scale of one to ten? About a four?' He ate about six grains of sticky Venetian *risotto nero* off the end of his fork, then made his fingers into a tentacle squid shape and flew them away from his plate across the table, blowing a childish raspberry noise with his tongue.

'Too much advance prep. Dead giveaway.' He made his mouth into a pink pout. 'Too much foreplay. Much better fresh and hot, wouldn't you say?'

They'd done a succession of *cicchetti* bars before dinner, and he was already quite sloshed.

His naked foot crept up her leg under the table and she saw the nice elderly waiter watching them. He was standing by the kitchen serving hatch and he lifted one of his bushy grey eyebrows at her, just like their editor Bob did, then turned and shouted something into the kitchen, '*La bionda*!' needless to say, what else?

A sweaty cook's grinning face appeared at the hatch. They were making lewd jokes, of course. But they didn't know who he was, the flirty man with his toes making squiddly progress up her calf. They didn't know he was writing his review notes on the menu he'd asked to keep as a souvenir.

'*Come oggetto! Ricordo! Souvenir*!' Waving it and laughing.

'*Chris*topher!'

'So – the big question.' He was giving her a moist look while he filled their wine glasses.

Her heart gulped in her chest. She felt the blush invade her neck and face. God, he was awful. He was pursing his lovely top lip into the wine and the liquid glistened on his tongue when he smiled at her with his mouth a little open.

'The *big* question, Christopher?' Surely the fool wasn't going to propose to her!

'You're blushing!' he exclaimed, thrilled. His eyes usually watered when he laughed, as though crying and laughing came just as easily to him. As though all his emotions were impulsive, tender, vulnerable. He wiped away a tear with the corner of his napkin. 'Blushing!'

Then he put a serious expression on his face. She saw him do it deliberately, as if he were acting. But he was acting the acting. The effect was a bit mocking.

'Yes, the big question, my little quail.'

She waited. So did his foot under the table. So did the waiter and the cook, who'd noticed something was up. They were watching what was happening expectantly. They looked happy and proud – proprietorial – as if their restaurant and their food had been responsible for romance.

'What are we going to call you?' he asked.

What to call Christopher Hare's accessory?

He leaned across the table and took her hand. His eyes had filled up again. That was maybe why he didn't see the God-awful icy chill that followed her blush. Her face felt stiff suddenly, and there was a kind of ringing in her ears when he said, 'What about *Thé Glacé*? That seems perfect. Pale and cool and, oh my God, so . . .'

The creeping toes again.

When he came in to their hotel room a couple of hours after she got back, she pretended to be asleep. She could hear him trying not to breathe loudly while he undressed.

He'd be leaving his clothes all over the floor. In the bathroom he tried to pee without making any noise as well. He pissed like a cart-horse and his attempts to hush it up were just comical. Any other time it would have made her laugh out loud. Then he crept into bed and didn't come anywhere near her. He could be sweet like that, too, so surprised and sorry, making it up to her, ashamed and crestfallen, really sincere.

But oh, what a kissy little shit sometimes.

Don't say she hadn't been warned.

Later during the night she woke up and heard him trying hard to breathe really quietly again. She knew what he was doing – the bed wobbled. Typical, all about him, just like at the restaurant where he'd sat sulking while she stormed out and found her own way back to the hotel through all those dark alleyways, past slurping backwater canals.

In the morning when she woke up he was lying as far away from her as possible, looking at her with puppy-dog eyes and a pout, ashamed, apologetic, indecisive. His hair was sticking up in tangled clumps. A narrow stripe of bright sunlight crossed his stupidly hairy bare chest like the sash of a uniform.

He looked ridiculous. She could see the words 'I'm *really* sorry' taking shape in his expression so she smacked him as hard as she could across the face. Just walloped him with her best tennis arm.

Don't you dare tell me you're sorry.

She didn't say the words but he saw them. He kept his eyes wide and waited. There was a kind of ticking noise from the sunlit wall of their room as it began to heat up, as though the world outside had a secret it had to tell them in code. But now he wasn't silencing his apology any more, he was trying to stop a grin from getting out. She'd made a big red mark on his cheek, good riddance.

'You horrid little spoiled brat,' she hissed at him, daring him to smirk. 'You self-fucking-important little shit. You *wanker.*'

His grin began to emerge so she smacked him again, hard, with the flat of her hand, twice, in the middle of the sun-stripe on his ridiculous hairy chest. He yelled and pushed his red bottom lip out, like a child about to cry. But he was laughing, really.

The Christopher memories. Sucking all the air out of the present. 'Food is love.' Try 'food is shit' for a change.

Could we be much closer if we tried
We could stay at home and stare into each other's eyes

'You sat there all wrapped up in your own fucking big question moment and let me find my own way back. In the dark. What an utter shit.'

'I did not,' he purred. He was trying to soothe her, but he was also a bit offended. And his eyes were flicking down at her body under the sheet.

'Don't even think about it, shit-face.'

'I followed you all the way back here. I hid. I crept from shadow to shadow. You didn't even know I was there.'

How could she tell if he was lying? She couldn't. They lay in silence, staring at each other. He wasn't smirking any more. He had that serious look she knew. When he licked his lips like that, little flicks of his tongue, she knew what was going to happen.

Then of course they just rushed together, as usual. He was all over her with his kissy mouth until it was unbearable and she had to scream. Scream! Then they were fucking and he had that expression, jubilant, his whole body laughing not just his face. Laughing and laughing. So he never did apologise for the 'big question' quarrel.

'Don't say I didn't warn you,' was what Bob said when she told him what had happened after they got back to London. 'You're *what*?'

'We're getting married.'

Not as if Bob hadn't warned her off him the first time they'd met at the magazine's offices in Thurloe Place. *A wide boy*, Bob had said, wagging his finger. *Watch out. Trouble.* They could hear Bob's latest discovery Christopher Hare rushing up the stairs. He was late.

'South Kensington!' he exclaimed as he stuck his big curly head around the door of Bob's office. He was panting from climbing up two flights. 'This is different. Wow.'

She recognised the New Zealand accent.

'The Brompton Oratory,' he said, rounding his vowels mockingly. 'The V and A!'

Was he a Maori? He had black curly hair and was either tanned or dark. A bit Maori, as it turned out. The rest was Italian.

He flopped down in a chair and fanned himself with a magazine. His quick scan of the room took her in – and waited. When Bob introduced them he jumped up clumsily and shook her hand, which was a nice change, after the cheek-kissing craze.

But when he left after the meeting he did kiss her cheek and made a little plosive sound with it, pop! – quite sweet.

'Lovely,' he crooned, so matinée-idol. 'Looking forward to it.'

He had a slightly leathery smell; she couldn't place it. Horse sweat? Maybe he went riding? But later she found it was just his smell.

Wily old Bob had spotted him, a journeyman chef turned 'junket journalist'. He was getting gigs with travel guides, churning it out for in-flight magazines, doing promos for hotel restaurants. Working miles and miles off the shoulder of the high end when he was on the road by himself on his own budget, getting new places all the time and talking them up – how did he find them?

That was where his buzz came from, especially around the Ligurian coast. He'd practically rewritten it. With respect and affection.

But cheerfully taking advantage of the prestige regulars when there was a junket available. She read his stuff – very funny, pithy and shameless – and she'd looked forward to meeting him.

When he was getting paid to promote he didn't hide it, he even boasted about the luxury, and when he wasn't promoting he was fearless. He'd had a field day making fun of Frank Sinatra's favourite Genoese restaurant Zeffirino, his story filling the place with furtive, superannuated bodyguards whose heads were permanently wrenched sideways watching the entries and exits.

He described the famed Zeffirino *paffutelli* as 'muck'. He told a silly story about Tom Hanks panting up the cliff from a wealthy businessman's yacht wanting to use the pool at Hotel Splendido in Portofino and being told to *vaffanculo!*

But oh my God, even with all that gossipy nonsense, when he wrote about the food and the wine you wanted to be there. You wanted to be there *with him*.

You wanted to be *in his mouth*.

A few words, a little taste of this and another of that, precise, clear, no jargon, how good was the kitchen, where did the prep set its freshness frontier, was the management calm, *what would you always remember*. And always just a bit naughty. He told jokes. He had fun. He knew what he was writing about. He had the magic tongue. The buds.

And there was a bit of a cult thing happening with him, as with Kiwi and Australian chefs, and that grassy Sauvignon Blanc when it first turned up.

And as Bob said, with 'the colonials', it was all care and no responsibility for the magazine – take the credit and disclaim the blame if things went bad. With them it was no connections and no loyalty. Just pure naked ambition and greed or better still an attitude. He gave them two years max before they locked in and got too compromised if they were any good.

A couple of months at most if they didn't perform.

But oh, Christopher Hare. A different story.

Playing Joe Jackson again. 'Pretty woman out walking with gorillas down my street.' To drown out 'Food is love.'

*

He was lying on his back and might even have been asleep. In the bathroom mirror she looked thoroughly ravaged.

The first time it happened was in a crappy cheap six-berth sleeper somewhere along the summer holiday coast from Ventimiglia. Fleeing the dreadful things he did to Robuchon's caramelised quail in Monaco. A whole family got out of the sleeper and left them to it around midnight, at some little beach-front town with a summer fairground and an illuminated merry-go-round with raucous amplified music and naked coloured lightbulbs along the beach, still going strong that late.

It had been going to happen for days, it was inevitable. The pressure building. They just jumped on each other as the train groaned and jerked out of the station leaving the little family yelling at one another over suitcases.

Then they drank two of the sample bottles of *Rossese di Dolceacqua* they were meant to be taking back to Bob in London and tried again, but he was too drunk and gave up.

They watched a dreary, flat, light industrial landscape chug past as dawn came up. The wretched Italian thing of rustic scraps and broken-down farm houses surrounded by ugly rubber mat factories or something. Streams of speeding cars overtaking the train, a purple band of nasty smog at the horizon.

'How can a place that makes such great food do this kind of shit?' He threw another empty bottle out the window with reckless abandon and hurt his elbow on the sill, bled all over the place. She was incredibly happy even though her cunt was sore after his hopeless drunken efforts.

He looked as though he was, too – happy that is. But really it was hard to tell. His default was 'be happy', and maybe that was sad in itself. Maybe his happiness was the saddest thing about him.

'You didn't!' scolded Bob the moment he saw her back

in the office. 'You can't do that!' He wasn't referring to the wine.

But for God's sake, it wasn't just Christopher. It was her, too. My God, was it ever. You couldn't blame Christopher.

And when Bob had looked at her photographs from that first trial trip he didn't even pause to think.

'You two,' he said, but not to Christopher, because you couldn't trust the bugger. 'Magic. It's a book. It's a fucking small fucking fortune!'

Magic.

Back in Venice the morning after the 'big question' debacle she threw cold water all over her face and head and shoulders and then walked back into the hotel bedroom without drying herself, with her hair dripping soothingly across her shoulders. The band of sunlight had spread and he now lay in the middle of it, as if on display. His long, skinny, impossible legs. He still had one sock on. It had a hole in it with his big toe sticking out. When she bent over him on the bed she thought it was her drips at first, but it wasn't. The tears were running from his closed eyes into his ears.

'What am I supposed to do about it!' he sobbed. 'What am I supposed to do about this . . .' He lifted both hands and whacked himself on the chest once, twice, three times. 'This . . . *feeling!*'

When he squawked '*feeling!*' his mouth sprayed saliva. Something burst inside him and turned his mouth and lips into a fleshy volcano.

One part of her thought he was being a dickhead, loathsome, melodramatic and pathetic. The other part put her hand over his bubbling mouth and lay down beside him. Long and cool and pale. His Thé Glacé if that's what he wanted. It didn't really matter.

'For God's sake, Christopher. It's okay. Stop being such a wet. I'll be your Thé Glacé if it'll make you shut up. Can we stop the performance and get some breakfast?'

He was gazing at her with a weak, grateful grin, blinking teary eyes.

'TG for short, okay? Can we start with a Campari Spritz? It's traditional. Then scrambled eggs with salmon.'

You couldn't blame Christopher. She mixed the drinks. They sat with no clothes on by the window in the sunshine, cracking jokes, knowing there was going to be another crisis to get through somewhere just a bit further along from where they were, probably not very far. Believing they could do it. Live for the moment.

The eggs arrived and he opened the door and collected them, no tip, still naked. She could picture his grin.

But then he didn't eat them. He drank the coffee in a gulp and started writing in his Moleskine notebook, making funny chewy expressions with his mouth. She got dressed and went out to take some pictures of fish in the Rialto market, leaving him to it. Quite probably he was writing about the mediocre *risotto nero* in the dump where they'd had their 'big question' row, and the eggs he'd only tasted and fiddled with. Making up a story with something silly like Lord Byron's favourite hangover cure in it – which was hock and soda, but –

'. . . of course you know that. Yeah, Thé Glacé, she knows everything about everything. Don't you, TG, you little crème brûlée?'

She thought about him as she took the photographs – his maddening combination of indifference and excess. She photographed a glistening pile of little cuttlefish sheaths with tentacled mouths. There were piles of bright-eyed sardines and anchovies, arranged facing the same way like a shoal. Once it would have been their pattern that attracted her – their *design*. Now it was their urgency.

The flushed colour in a tray of red mullet was almost hectic; it seemed to be coming from inside, under pressure. A shouting man dumped a sack of black hairy mussels into a bin in front of her, splashing her camera with seawater. Later she would see his wet bare arms reaching into her picture as if to embrace her.

She forgot about Christopher and went on taking pictures. She ate a paper plate of *fritto misto* with a glass of rather turpentiney white wine because she was hungry, which meant quite a lot of time had passed since breakfast.

Then she saw Christopher's head in his faded red baseball cap bobbing above the crowd. He was periscoping around, looking for her. That unmistakable little jolt in her groin, a kind of thickening in her throat.

She'd been doing something different, taking the photographs, and along with the sexy feeling when she saw Christopher came another ping of excitement, maybe related, maybe not.

He saw her and pushed through the crowd to where she was standing by the *fritto* booth. Looking a bit sulky, he reached across and took a helping of the fries. As usual, he waited until they were in his mouth before talking to her.

'Having fun, are we?'

'As a matter of fact.'

He took a sip of her wine and grimaced. 'How can you drink that shit?'

But next he was grinning again, of course, his lips oily from her snack. His cap was perched on top of those thick curls. They stuck out over his ears. When she didn't play he looked alarmed. She could tell that he was about to apologise again.

She took his picture – looking indecisive, with a kind of default grin, needing a shave, his eyes a bit watery. His mouth had begun to form a word, 'sorry' probably, but the photograph stopped it before he could speak, freezing his lips on a pout.

Behind him was a blurry crowd of people in the market, glimpses of coloured fruit and vegetables, splashes of sunlight. The noisy place seemed to have gone quiet, its bustle motionless like a sudden, surprising thought.

It was obvious. The photograph of Christopher marked the moment when she asked herself her own 'big question'. The answer was in the photographs she took at the market, or the way she took them. That had something to do with Christopher, his effect on her, how she looked at things, something instinctive. He freed it up.

But then, as well, it didn't. It also didn't have anything to do with him at all.

'You've gone off somewhere. What are you thinking about?'

'Sensation,' she replied. He wasn't going to understand that and she wasn't going to help him. She could see that he was casting about for a gambit.

'You wouldn't understand,' she said, finishing the wine he hadn't liked very much.

'Sensational.' He was trying very hard, but she had him worried. '*That* I understand, my little icecream.' He had that beseechy expression, he got it when she was being cool.

There were some places it was better not to go, and others you couldn't stay away from, but at least you could keep the curtains drawn.

Six months out of rehab again when she and Christopher first met at Bob's office, and late autumn in London was just utter shit, the beery yobs on the Underground made her flesh creep and so did the nasty muddy banks along the river by Wandsworth Park when the tide was out, filthy old barges, slime, beer cans. Dishevelled, malignant rooks being bored on the tidal mud-flats or croaking in the dreary trees, panicky ducks sticking their heads into the dirty Thames.

She walked and walked. What else was there to do but get high? Stupid old dogs shitting all over the grass, rich young Putney bitches running around and around in expensive gym shoes.

She was having a coffee in the High Street and looking out the window when she saw a happy young woman hurrying past with a huge wobbling cluster of coloured helium balloons advertising a Play Centre. She shocked even herself with the loud sobs that made her run into the street and hide around the corner, pulling her parka hood over her face.

What was she supposed to do? The thought of food revolted her and, as Bob said, she was taking pictures of it that looked about as appetising as wiring diagrams.

Taking pictures of people was even worse. She hated all of them. Their confidence and grooming, how they treated her like some kind of employee. Which she was.

If she stopped taking her Prozac she hated them and herself even more and longed for a decent taste. And if she took the wretched stuff she couldn't care less what the photographs looked like.

Of course, she could always trust dear old Bob to have a brilliant idea. Waving a clipping from the Sunday Times colour supplement at her. So what about a feature on those YBA artists showing at the Royal Academy? The *Sensation* exhibition? Didn't she go to art school with some of them? Their favourite restaurants maybe? Weren't they all filthy rich already?

Oh, right, she told Bob. That was going to make her feel ever so much better. The tragic one who ended up photographing the table settings at Peter Gordon's hot new Sugar Club in Notting Hill. Where, as it so happens, she saw Marcus Harvey being lavish with the collector Charles Saatchi and a bunch of old art school mates from Goldsmiths. Her not included. She used to party with Marcus, not long before she graduated, about ten years ago. Now, he didn't recognise her. Or pretended he didn't.

But she went along to the exhibition. The work everyone was making a fuss about, aside from Damien's pickled shark and Tracey Emin's fuck tent, was Marcus Harvey's portrait of

Myra Hindley. The 'child killer'. There she was, her mugshot reproduced using hundreds of childrens' hand-prints, blonde and beautifully groomed under the weird helmet-like hairdo, high cheek-bones, that elegant, slightly smiling mouth, those candid eyes.

It was like looking into some kind of ghastly mirror.

No, she told Bob. She knew she hadn't made it. She was photographing the food not ordering it. But she wasn't going to rub her own face in the fact. Forget it. Not a chance.

'Well, we have to do something to buck you up.' Then, good old Bob, she saw him have another thought. The happy lightbulb went on behind his serious editor expression.

Christopher Hare. Christopher who?

By then it was nearly spring. Everyone seemed to be noticing that. There was a new season's edition to put together in time for summer. Bob had that last chance look. Hers, not the magazine's. The magazine was going through the roof.

But when she looked down into the viewfinder of her Rollei something heavy in the front of her skull slid forward and made her feel sick. When she looked straight ahead into the Nikon she either hesitated and shot, knowing she'd missed the moment, or she shot without thinking and knew the result would be dumb.

She was doing product-placement interiors and settings with Garnier Thiebaut table linens. Yet another authentic fucking vinegar crock with a spigot. A wine rack you can customise for that handy space under the stairs in Mayfair. Chromed meat hooks to hang your pots off and de Buyer pots to hang off them. Easter celebration ideas. Outdoor Entertaining, and chasing away the winter blahs.

'But no people, Bob – no food on plates. No one having fun.' Because when she pointed a camera at anything yummy her brains fell out. Because no one stayed in her bed any longer than it took to show them to the door before breakfast.

Because what was the point.

Thirty-two years old, trust fund frozen except for treatments, pokey flat on the dreary Wandsworth side of Putney.

She put on Elvis Costello. *Get Happy.*

'I can't stand up for falling down.'

Bob had handed her a folder of Christopher's clippings. 'Come on, sweetie. Have a look.' What he meant was, Or else try spending your day on a park seat not too far from the conveniences.

Six months without using but she scored on the way home. Did he really expect her to run around after some try-hard fucking New Zealander? The bag was pinkish because the coke was cut with raspberry flavouring. Everything had that trivial, try-hard look, even the drug.

What's it to be? Admit defeat or trot around after Christopher Nobody. And what's the difference, really? She made a tidy line on the kitchenette bench and got a nice little rush about the time she'd read to page six of the clippings folder.

The Jamaican couple in the flat below were having a row with their six-year-old, that was lively too, and when she laughed out loud she suddenly had to pause and find out why. Then they put on some skank music downstairs and after a while the little girl was laughing at what her daddy was doing to make her eat her dinner. He was being an elephant.

There were only a dozen more pieces to read and by the time she'd finished them she'd worked it out. The little family downstairs was funny and lively all right but she was noticing that because what she'd read was funny too. Did the coke have anything to do with it? Of course it did. But she flushed what was left away. Which was *really* hard, but what choice did she have? Christopher Who or Serenity Detox in Camden?

The decider was something he'd written about an obscure

Paris bistro called Le Baratin run by a female Italian-Argentinian chef. Le Baratin did beef cheeks braised slowly in syrah; how vile could you get? But her mouth flooded with saliva for the first time in months when Christopher Hare's jaunty five-hundred worder put a forkful of the meat in her mouth.

And that was what she'd seen when he came into the office in Thurloe Place. She *saw* how he'd slowly closed his lips around the meat and then pressed it with his teeth, feeling its succulent texture while the juice poured out of it.

In Bob's office he had that jubilant, open-mouthed look – 'Brilliant, brilliant!' – but then his face would get sleepy, almost sullen, chewing those tasty lips. His gaze clouded over or out of focus, or looking inward.

She asked him about Le Baratin and the cheeks. When he said '*joues de boeuf*', his Frenching lips made the absurd, exaggerated shape of a wet, pouting sea-anemone. When that made her laugh she covered her own mouth with her hand. Then realised what she'd done. As if her mouth could ever look as utterly naked as Christopher's.

'We'll go there! First stop!'

Bob's bushy left eyebrow went up.

The other thing about Christopher was his legs. He was taller than average, but not when he was sitting down. That was because his legs were out of proportion with the rest of him. They were long and skinny. Excessively hairy, she found out later. The waistbands of his off-the-rack trousers were always too big, so he had to pull them in with a belt, but they always looked baggy. And then he'd sit down and seem at once to shrink, because his torso was short by comparison.

In Bob's office, his legs had stuck out and got in his way. He was wearing huge scuffed Australian Blundstones. Then, the first time she saw him sit down behind a table – she'd asked for Peter Gordon's new Sugar place in Soho – she laughed because he seemed to shrink dramatically.

'What?' he demanded. That sulky look.

'How did you do that? Fold yourself down?'

He was glaring at her.

'Sorry, is it a sore point? I mean, you . . .' She made a sliding movement with her hand. Then he kicked her under the table, not hard, but just the same. Their first time out together, pre-assignment, getting to know each other.

'Oh, sorry,' he grinned. Next thing he was happily cracking jokes with chef Gordon. Whom he knew, of course, 'another brilliant Kiwi'.

'I'll tell you what the trouble is, Peter, cherub,' he was drawling. 'It doesn't look like food any more. It looks like fucking art. Sensational art, but art.'

He didn't know what he'd just said, then, but she kicked him back anyway.

'Oh, sorry,' she mimicked.

He and Peter Gordon looked a bit alike, curly-haired, mischievous. The chef was staring at her, trying to remember if he'd seen her before. He had, as a matter of fact, at the Notting Hill place. Photographing the table-settings. Then he turned and hurried back to his kitchen. Her point, exactly.

Back outside the restaurant, a bit drunk, Christopher bent to tickle the head of a miniature Dachshund on a young man's lap, and the dog snapped at him. He pretended to flee into the posh Soho Sanctum hotel next door. She couldn't decide if he was an embarrassing show-off or actually amusing.

The next morning, she was sitting in the Paris train as it was about to depart when she saw his red baseball cap bobbing urgently along above the stragglers on the platform. He'd made sandwiches for both of them because the buffet food was 'complete shit'.

When they got off the train, his suitcase sprang open in the concourse at the Gare du Nord. She stuffed handfuls of his wrinkled clothes into her bag – that horse-leathery smell.

'Thanks, pal,' he said. He didn't seem to have embarrassment in his nature.

He hadn't booked at Le Baratin but the owners made an arrangement when they saw him. She photographed the chef Raquel with a plate of her *joues de boeuf*; also the jolly interior of the restaurant.

'Food is love.' Christopher told her a rambling story about his Italian grandmother back in New Zealand. '*Food is love, Christopher*, she would say. *And don't you forget it*.'

Food is love.

Obviously he fancied her. He fell asleep on the Metro and put his big woolly head on her shoulder in the hotel lift. But she closed her door in his grinning face and sat on a chair by the open window. She thought she might be feeling happy. The air from the hotel's courtyard wasn't very fresh and a man was snoring in a nearby room. It was all quite vivid. Something encouraging seemed to be happening. The beef cheeks had been delicious but not nearly as good as reading about them or watching Christopher say their name.

Moments after she took the first photograph of Raquel beaming above the plate of glistening meat and carrots she had a *sensation*. A vivid little shuttering in her mind, a just-right sensation.

When she turned the tap on to brush her teeth back at the hotel, the ancient plumbing groaned loudly; she laughed as she spat the winey taste of their meal. The skinny, shirt-button-breasts leek of a woman in the scruffy hotel mirror didn't look anything like Myra Hindley in Marcus Harvey's ghastly painting, the child killer's smug meaningless smirk, not candour but a kind of sightlessness in her stare, the primped, sticky hair. The woman in the mirror was smiling as if that was what she always did.

When she looked for a T-shirt to go to bed in she found she still had some of Christopher's stuff in her bag. Of course she didn't put one of his on, but the thought crossed her mind, and she remembered the way Bob's big grey eyebrow had gone up, back in Thurloe Place.

And yes, she had a quick sniff at it.

They caught the train to Nice. She made Christopher buy a cheap new trundly suitcase at the Gare de Lyon. He repacked at a table outside the station café. When the waiter chased him with the old empty one he parked it by a rubbish bin and walked away backwards, blowing kisses and waving to it.

'Au revoir, chérie, tu ne m'en veux pas? Regarde, ma nouvelle biquette!'

'Biquette?'

'Little she-goat.' He put a hand to his mouth in mock dismay. 'Sorry, no offense.'

So, probably, that was how it started, the whole thing, sensational. The whole catastrophe.

The memories. Can't live with them, can't live without them.

But, *maya.yazbeck@hotmail*? Who was Maya Yazbeck? Why was Christopher sending a message with her email?

Costello singing: *Simple though love is, still it confused me.*

'Message from your husband.'

Since when did he ever say that?

Food is love.

CHAPTER 3

Yes, of course, she could see that he was stupid – what, was she herself stupid as well? His indecision, his docility, but then his impulsive actions and his anger, these were unstable and she would say that they were the signs of an unstable personality. 'Stupid' was an easy way to describe this and for the driver Mahfouz that was sufficient. The food writer man was 'as stupid as a turd' and so forth, as usual, of course. She did not disagree.

And also, of course, as Mahfouz and the others did not need to tell her, it was the stupid turds that were the most dangerous. Why? Because they did stupid actions. Therefore, there was no question. The stupid turd from the restaurant would have to be shot. Yes, of course they were right, that was why they were being patient with her. It was a matter of time. When had there ever been a good reason to hesitate over such a thing? Unlike the taxi, the idiot who had jumped into it could not have his colour or his number-plate changed. He could not turn from a white taxi into the red saloon of the importer of cheap Turkish furniture and leather shoes.

Tomorrow morning, unlike the taxi, he would be the same – white, obvious, with a sign on the top of his head and an identification number on his arse! He would still be stupid and, being stupid, he would still be dangerous. He might as well drive himself around the city with a loudspeaker! Therefore.

Thus, Mahfouz. Of course. But then, the food writer was also not stupid. She had seen from Google that he was also quite famous – indeed, he had written a book about *Arabian Nights: 1,001 Middle Eastern Feasts*. That did not seem very likely, but however. And unlikely also that the famous food writer's book mentioned the UNRWA beans and rice or canned Kraft cheese they ate in Baqa'a refugee camp.

And, in some part, he was also not afraid. That, of course, could be another sign of stupidity. But it could also mean that he had a purpose of some kind, though perhaps he did not know it. Perhaps he did not yet understand his direction. It was as though he had been drawn after her by the force of her mission, though he was ignorant of its purpose. And also, if he was merely stupid, he would not be interesting. This Christopher Hare was interesting – stupid and therefore dangerous, yes, but also there was something happening in his mind that he was becoming aware of, and that was interesting. He said he was bored – that made him interesting. His decision to jump in the taxi was interesting, it was an instinct that came from his boredom. Really stupid people were not bored, only people with intelligence. He did not understand it, his decision, but perhaps she could help him with his understanding. What did he know about the present situation in Baqa'a, in Rafah, in Amman New Camp? In Homs, in Ain el-Hilweh? In Shatila? What they ate there, in the camps? Nothing, certainly. What he vomited upstairs did not come from the *carte du jour* at Shatila.

'So now, you see, he is empty,' she said to them. 'You heard it. Now, we can fill him up.'

'Now he is full of shit!' That was Mahfouz the driver, needless to say. But then he had to finish with the taxi, and anyway, he did not matter, Mahfouz. He went out the back, cursing, to do his work in the truck garage. 'Don't waste time! Shoot the son of a shit-pants whore now and be done with it! Then we sink him in the harbour for the crabs to eat his shit!'

That left Philippe the older, quiet one – he was drinking a glass of water and watching her with patience. He was tapping with one fingernail against the glass and sucking the water from his moustache with his bottom lip. His eyelids were going up and down very slowly. It was already agreed that the two of them decided, it had to be unanimous, whatever it was that was happening.

'But you also shot the woman,' Philippe said quietly. They were eating slices of pita bread with warm oil and thyme and she was drinking a glass of tea. 'I already heard it from Antun at the restaurant, before he talked to the police.' He wagged the cellphone that was close to his glass of water. Then he resumed tapping on the glass. Tap, tap, tap. 'So now, you see, we have three problems, not one.'

'No,' said Hawwa. She admired Philippe and trusted him, but there was always the question of leadership. 'Now we have one problem, Philippe, and that is how you and I will agree.'

'Let me explain.' He leaned across the table and counted what he was saying with his piece of pita. 'How it seems to me, in my opinion only, you understand. Number one, we have your friend upstairs who has become so infatuated he had to jump in the taxi with you. Then, we have the fact that you shot the whore of Abdul Yassou, for which I can't blame you, but we didn't agree to do that.'

'And number three?' He would already see that she did not enjoy his patronising manner.

He put his piece of bread down on the table and took a sip of water. Sometimes he liked to go very slowly, Philippe – he was sucking his moustache again. 'Number three, Oum Boutros,' he murmured, putting a knife in her heart with that mention of her son, 'is that I fear you and I will not agree about this matter of your friend upstairs before Antun gets here, which will be in the morning after he is sure the police have not followed him and after he has not had a good night's sleep. It is a question of timing. At this moment this obliging maître d' is talking to the police and sending them in the wrong direction. But he will be very angry and afraid because you shot the woman and also because of the complication with the stupid man who has become infatuated. So, trust me, when Antun gets home after the police he will not be sleeping, and when he gets here he will want to hear a good decision. One that will help him with his fear. With his future.'

Hawwa watched her friend Philippe consider how he was going to say the next thing – the important part. She already had a sense of what it could be. While she was waiting, she was noticing that the place was disorderly. The cups and plates had not been washed recently, there were cigarette butts that had not been cleaned away, and there was a smell of scorched chickpeas, as if someone had forgotten that a pot was cooking on the gas burner. All this was careless and not like Philippe, who was in charge of the house.

'What,' he said, mildly, catching the direction of her survey, 'you think some dirty Arab truck drivers are going to keep a maid in their house to clean up their mess? A cook, perhaps, as well? You spend too much time in Geneva, my friend. When we are gone, we the truck drivers, that is all they will notice, the ones who come to clean up. As usual, the filth. The "Arab filth".'

But this was trivial. He leaned forward and touched the back of her hand respectfully with one finger, the one that had his wedding band on it. 'What of course you know, Hawwa, my comrade, is that when you shot the woman of Abdul Yassou, for which who could blame you, but without our agreement, you placed yourself in debt. You placed yourself in debt to me, your comrade, in the terms of our agreement. Now let us say you owe me a life. Surely you can see that this must be the life of your new friend who even now is beginning to think what he should do, upstairs?

That is not only the honorable thing in the terms of our agreement, it is also the sensible thing, and it is what Antun will expect to have happened when he comes here tomorrow morning with a fear about the police and about the well-known friends of Abdul Yassou making him unreliable also. Or angry in the way that will make him ask for more money to stop him going to talk to somebody. Or perhaps he will talk, anyway, to save his skin. You see how this new friend of yours upstairs has begun to unpick a thread at the end of our blanket so that soon we will all be uncovered.'

Yes, it was true. She remembered the look of disbelief and rage that was not play-acting on the maître d' Antun's face as she left the restaurant where the screaming had begun to mix with the sounds of chairs falling over. She saw in an instant that Antun did not know what to do. And then, he had not stopped the fool from chasing after her down the stairs. Why not? Because he did not know what to do but also because he did not know how to act. He was incapable. So who was more dangerous – Antun, whom the police might already have seen was a man with a nervous problem, or Christopher the food writer upstairs here in the 'truck drivers' house' whom the same police might conclude was a zealous member of the public? Whom the gangsters had kidnapped? More likely, who had simply run away, quite sensible under the circumstances? Leaving behind no credit card details, since he had not paid? So who was he? Certainly, the police knew who Abdul Yassou was, and good riddance. Perhaps they would be glad to see the last of him. And now, they also knew who Antun was, the maître d' with a nervous disposition.

'Yes, Philippe, of course you are right,' she said, moving her hand away from his finger. Inside her chest her heart was thudding strongly and she knew she would have to try hard to keep her breath calm. 'But let me ask you a question, since you have given me the benefit of your thoughts.'

He inclined his head a little, courteously. He would always

be calm. 'Of course, bint Habash.' *Daughter of Habash* – another knife in her heart. First the wound of her dead son, then that of her dead father. Yes, this was the way Philippe did it.

'Yes, I am a Habash, as you unnecessarily remind me – and like my father's cousin al-Hakim, I prefer to look at the whole *tric trac* board before I move a piece. That is what George used to say, as you surely remember, Philippe. No doubt you heard him say it, that other Habash, that George, that al-Hakim.'

'Another piece,' murmured Philippe. 'Yes, he did say something like that, from time to time. He used to say, keep something back, a piece, behind the line, to be a nuisance. I think I heard him, may he rest in peace. He lived a very long time.' Philippe crossed himself but without emotion, and she had to wonder if he was trying to provoke her.

'Let me ask you, then, simply, which of the fool upstairs or the fool from the restaurant who is even now talking to the police do you think is the more dangerous? Since I am, as you say, in your debt?'

The older man looked at her without changing his expression, but his finger stopped tapping on his glass of water. They both noticed that an acrid smell of spray paint had crept into the room. So, Mahfouz was about his work, back in the truck garage. Soon, the white taxi would be a red saloon and he would fill the back seat with boxes of badly printed Turkish brochures – leather shoes without feet in them, as if their owners had gone to pray, or to their graves.

Philippe smiled at her, which did not mean he was feeling happy or friendly. He sniffed the chemical air that was coming from the truck garage. 'So, you see, how good we are, you and I, things proceed as they should.' Then he gestured with his eyebrows and chin towards the grey wig that was still on her head – yes, he had caught her out; with the fuss about the food writer she had forgotten to take it off.

She could not stop herself, she quickly put her hand up to her hair – the person she felt then was not who she was – she touched, for a moment only, a fool, the same one Philippe had pointed to mockingly with his chin. Philippe stood up carefully with a little grunt and dropped the cellphone into his shirt pocket. 'I will clean, up there,' he said, and went towards the stairs.

All right. Of course it was unusual that he would do that, a man who made things *proceed as they should*. But he did not expect her to do it, that was part of his meaning. So, what was she to do? She sat with an image of her father's cousin George Habash's old fingers hesitating over the backgammon board. But not hesitating for long, ever. No, not hesitating – *thinking*. Seeing the whole board. Seeing all the time the game would take. Its past, its present moment, its future.

Upstairs in the bathroom Philippe was sluicing the food writer's vomit into the lavatory with the shower hose. She reached up and took the wig off her head. Thank God she was alone to do this, a kind of indecency. But then, a lightness. All this time after the restaurant she had been wearing it. It lay ridiculously on the table in front of her, like a dead cat. The sob that rose from her heavily beating heart burst out just once, a 'Huh!' that might have been her laughing at herself in the wig, except that a gush of tears also came out upon her cheeks. She saw again her husband Abdul Yassou jump and then sit down on the banquette, his eyes very wide, looking straight at her, while the blood suddenly poured out between the thick fingers around his neck.

There were some paper towels on the table with the pita bread and the oil, and she took one and wiped the tears from her eyes and cheeks. So, it was done. Finished. But now she had only a little time to finish the next thing. To make it happen as it should. To show Philippe the same respect he had given her – to clean up her own mess, before Antun arrived in the morning to see if they had taken his difficult situation into consideration and secured his future.

When did this catastrophe begin? She held an ache under her eye between her fingers. It seemed to reside in the little bag there. Perhaps now was a good time to begin to ask, rather, when might it stop?

But then, it seemed to her that this question about a beginning and an end was also like the question of the food writer upstairs – he who had begun by running away into a circumstance whose end was also at once certain and like a dream. This she understood. This at once reminded her. Every July in Amman as the weather began to get hotter and the *hamseen* winds continued intermittently to drive people into mad rages, Oum Musa her father's mother, rest her soul, used to bring down a box from the big mother-of-pearl inlaid Syrian cabinet in the hallway of the house. Or rather, she required her son to bring it down. The box resided in its own compartment, which Oum Musa approached, wailing, while her assembled grandchildren watched already knowing what was going to happen. But first the maid would have swabbed the *hamseen* dust from the hallway floor and covered the dining room table with an embroidered cloth for the box to sit on. Afterwards, in acknowledgement of the grandmother's emotion, and also that of her son and daughter-in-law – who were of course always present, having reserved the day in July for this commemoration – there would be tea with some lunch, and then Oum Musa would retire for her siesta which, on this day, would last until evening. And then, as the heat of the day thickened towards sunset, while the *imams* began to echo each other from the city's mosques, the old woman would ascend to the roof of the house on Jebel Ashrafieh and sit facing the dusty red haze of the setting sun to the west, in the direction of Lydda, of *al-Nakba*, the catastrophe of 1948, when Palestinians were first driven into exile by the Israelis. She wore the embroidered dress with the fine needlework bodice from her own wedding outfit, and a headscarf of Nazareth lace with birds and flowers.

Over there, beyond the horizon of the earth but not beyond that of her memory, on a small hill above the wide plain of Lydda in the neighbourhood around the Orthodox church, was the white-stone house built by her son when he married. It shared an old wall with a house of his wife's family and also a well of good water and an old garden. In the little garden were two orange trees and a grapevine whose trunk was the thickness of a girl's waist – yes, insisted the grandmother, the very thickness of her own waist when she first entered the house of her own marriage not so far away in Ramla. The front door of her son's wedding house was made of iron and came from an old house of her husband's family in Ramla. Her own brothers and their cousins, her son's uncles, brought it to Lydda on a wagon when her son's house was finished. The priest who had married them blessed it with holy water, and then walked into the house through the iron door, sprinkling water down the hallway and with smoking *lubbān* from the church's great swinging thurible. In the keystone above the iron door was a finely chiselled *Mar Jiryis* so that Saint George might protect the house, God willing. The new walls were inset with deep windows which, on the ground floor, had decorative bars of fine iron-work on the outside. This was a large house with four rooms upstairs and four down, an outhouse, a bathhouse with a copper for heating water, and a cookhouse with a brick oven used also by the neighbours – a larger house than most of those around it, which was noticed and respected, thank God, because the families were prosperous and also because her son was a dentist to the wealthy as far away as Jaffa and Haifa, as well as the owner of orange orchards and of trade interests in the port of Jaffa.

So went the dirge of Hawwa's grandmother on the rooftop while her daughter-in-law hovered with a towel moistened with water and eau-de-cologne. Afterwards, when the sun had set and the sky emptied of darting swallows, the grandmother would go to mass and light candles for Saint George to remember that it was his *Mar Jiryis* above the door of the house in Lydda.

Even as a little girl, Hawwa saw that her father allowed her grandmother precedence in all of this – but after she died the box was no longer taken down from the Syrian chest, though it still resided there. Because, her father said, we have to occupy the present with as much determination as the Israeli Moishe Dayan's Lehi occupied Lydda and Ramla – may those Lehi rot in hell – and not sit waiting for any Arab to save us. And especially not those *fedayeen* fools who think that by blowing themselves up in Israeli minefields they will change what fate is already designing for them. Even the Maronite Phalangi, those Kataeb, are better than those fools of *fedayeen* though most of them are crooks and the sons of crooks and the enemies of Palestine. Over this he argued bitterly with her brothers and also especially with his cousin George Habash.

But not, she remembered, with the young businessman Abdul Yassou when he came to live in their house as a guest from Beirut when the war started there in 1975, the son of his old friend and business partner in Lydda, because Abdul Yassou was busy cultivating the good will of her father and being careful how he looked at her, because she was only sixteen years old at that time when the Lebanon war started, while he was a grown man.

And later, it had to be said, her father quarrelled with her, his own daughter, though she thought that in his heart he might have been proud of her spirit, which he showed in indirect ways by boasting of her success to others so that word of it reached her in the form of their jealous spite.

But this 'spirit' that her father secretly loved was not entirely her own nor, certainly, that of her friends both

French and Arab at the medical school in Paris who fancied themselves to be *fedayeen* because they wore *keffiyeh* and espoused armed resistance while amusing themselves in the charming open spaces of the Buttes Chaumont. It was also the spirit of her grandmother, and she had quarrelled with her father partly because her memory of her grandmother's litany of white-stone houses, iron doors, the carved *Mar Jiryis*, keys, orange trees, grapevines, marriages and wedding embroideries was so strong she could not distinguish what she truly remembered from what she had been told. Because of course *al-Nakba* happened ten years before she was born. But because it was told over and over, it was as though she truly remembered the house in Lydda with a grapevine whose trunk was the thickness of a newly married girl's waist, and an iron door from the time of the Ottomans or even from before the time when Napoleon besieged Jaffa, for the love of God, when her grandmother told of an ancestor who had interceded with Napoleon on behalf of the town's Muslims. Or even, if her grandmother was to be believed, from the time of the Crusades.

And the wooden box which her father would have lifted down for his mother from the inlaid Syrian cabinet and carried to the table in the dining room in the house of exile in Amman – it was always the same, throughout her childhood in that house for as long as her grandmother was alive: every year the grandmother would unlock the box, wailing, to reveal another key, a huge iron one with a long shaft. This was the key to the iron door of the white-stone house in Lydda. Also in the box were the deeds to the properties including the house and orchards. As well as the British Mandate deeds there was an old deed, unfolded every year with care along its creases that almost severed it into quarters, that had on it what she was told was the colophon of the Ottoman Sublime Porte. But more important even than that, insisted her grandmother with her hands laid flat on the old paper, so as to press it down and to feel its creases against her palms, was the thickness of the grapevine's trunk, which was older even than Napoleon. And had been planted by the family along with the orange groves over towards Jaffa.

So this was one 'beginning'. And so was what felt like a memory of those people the Israelis drove out of Lydda, the catastrophe in that July of 1948 commemorated by her grandmother, when so many died of thirst and heat and grief along the road to Barfiliya. Her own memory, which of course she could not truly claim, was of a rubbled white-stone wall made blinding by sunlight, and beside it a long, ragged column of people whose strong shadows told of the terrible heat of the sun. This was a photograph she had seen. She imagined her grandmother there, though in fact the family had left some weeks before, thank God, taking the deed box with the great key so as to be able to return when the fighting stopped and prove their ownership of whatever was left.

What kind of a 'beginning' and what kind of memory was this, truly? A photograph, and her grandmother's ritual? An image of a time before her birth, of a place her grandmother had not been in? Its truth was in how it had shaped her life, or, as it might be, how she had shaped her life with it. Yes – this she understood; she did not deceive herself.

And was the 'end' also in the deed box, which was still in the Amman house of her late father, now legally her older brother Habib's house, though it was she who lived there when not in Geneva, keeping company with the old key that would unlock the past before *al-Nakba* and allow that past to flow into a present in which she would return with her grandmother's memory to the white-stone house protected by Saint George on a small hill in Lydda whose iron door from perhaps before the Ottomans had by now, on the day of Abdul Yassou's death, been closed already for sixty years?

But of course the house was no longer there.

It was not in the present.

She knew this in the part of her that knew such things, which was not the same as the part that remembered the house and believed it, even though she had never seen it.

Yes, like the present moment of the crazy food writer whose impulse had trapped her into this responsibility for a decision she did not wish to make, she was trapped between a false memory and an impossible dream. Between a beginning that was authentic in the experience of her grandmother, but then, after all, not authentic in the same degree as the experience of those who had suffered on the long road to Barfiliya or, now, in the refugee camps to which they had bequeathed their children's children – because her grandmother and her mother and father and her older brothers had been luckier than the ones in the camps. Of course she also knew that her grandmother's 'performance' was one of the reasons her father had locked the box away when the old woman died. It was time he said to move forward not in denial of the past and its curses but in order to prove that the family did not have to be always the lamenting victim of an unjust fate. As his daughter the physician, of whose success he was prouder than he showed, was indeed proving, despite her disobedient behavior.

And the other side of the trap was the possibility of a false ending in which she jeopardised the safety of her comrades and those on whose behalf she had presumed to act in shooting her own husband, Abdul Yassou, who had first looked at her from beneath his long eyelashes with such secret but to her apparent thoughts from the other side of the table in her father's house, where her grandmother was wailing as she unlocked the wooden box, when she, Hawwa, was a girl of sixteen whose own waist was the circumference of a grapevine in Lydda.

*

And what was the food writer's present moment – this stupid, stupid Christopher Hare who looked at her with such dumb, dreaming hope of some future, God knows what, some liberation? He had run out after something – not after her, despite Philippe's careful sarcasm. Or had run away from something, though hardly something like the Israeli butcher Dayan's Lehi driving jeeps into Lydda with guns blazing. This Christopher Hare had been driven from a paradise that may never have existed except as a false memory, and now perhaps he wished to return to something like it, although, like her grandmother's, his key was now useless. Or perhaps he saw a future unfolding from his actions. But what?

Perhaps he was even stupid enough to hope that *she*, Hawwa Habash, held the key to his future? She heard her own grunt of dismay and derision in the empty, foul-smelling room – and at the same time felt a familiar pang of unwelcome compassion.

She had seen an expression of stupid expectation like Christopher Hare's on the faces of men and women in l'Hôpital Robert Debré, in the foyer of the *urgences pédiatriques*, when she came out in her white coat that was like a uniform of false hope and inauthentic authority, to tell them that their child's kidneys were, indeed, sadly, failing, or that the beautiful, trembling, miniature pump in their baby's chest was not assembled correctly, or that this long delay in uttering language was the result of a mental impairment, or that, unfortunately, there was indeed this problem of white blood cells, and so on and so forth. And in the camps that had by now become towns and cities, in Burj el-Barajneh and Ain el-Hilweh and Beddawi in Lebanon, in Dera'a and Homs and the others in Syria, in Baqa'a and Irbid and Zarqa and Jerash in Jordan, in Shu'fat, al-Arroub, Jenin on the West Bank, in Jabalia and Rafah, Khan Yunis and Deir al-Balah and the rest in Gaza, in all of these and many other camps, as well as in the conference rooms of UNRWA in Gaza City and the WHO in Geneva, she had seen this same expression of absurd hope, however concealed by pride or deceit, sometimes a hope that she would be able to accomplish some kind of miracle, to repair the little trembling heart pump or provide proper food for the rickety child of the camps; at other times that she would be able to assist in the promulgation of a suitable lie, to defend the disbursements of UNRWA, for example, when they seemed to have become diminished in their passage through the hands of men such as Abdul Yassou.

Yes, to occupy this present moment and to act in it, leaving aside her father's ranting about Dayan, which after all came from his broken heart. That was the necessary thing. To see the whole board with both hers and the food writer's pieces on it. And also to make him play, because she would not consent to take his passive fate in her hands, which were already full.

Yes, it was her father's cousin George, that famous al-Hakim, that cunning strategist and leader, who had showed her and Philippe the trick of keeping a piece back on the *tric trac* board, to make the enemy hesitate and become defensive, and then to strike fast at the last minute and finish it. Slow, then fast, and always measuring the distance. Having it in your mind. 'Uncle George', smiling under his moustache, but with those large direct eyes of the Habash family not smiling, moving his arms and shoulders as if dancing rather than firing a gun.

That was in the year before the events of September in 1970 in Amman that drove George and his PFLP militias from the city. Yes, she was a child then, and remembered only the rattling sound of gunfire before dawn, in June, when the *fedayeen* and the Bedouin began to fight, and her father and brothers ran to close all the shutters so that when dawn came it remained dark in the house, and for many days. The electricity that came and went, the smell of cooking on the small paraffin stove. And again, in the second part of the fighting, in September, when Wasfi al-Tal implemented his massacre with the tanks.

But she also remembered, long past the time of her childhood, how it would be argued over and over, and not least at the time of al-Hakim's funeral almost four decades later in the very city from which he and his PFLP had been driven out, whether that expulsion was because he lost the game, or whether he merely lost a battle in the longer war – whether he kept something back, as was his habit. Whether he saw that inevitable outcome in 1970, too, when his fighters were driven out of Jordan and into Lebanon, and won something in the end. As Philippe was not slow to remind her, George Habash had died an old man, in the city of his former enemy, that Bedouin Hussein; he had won the war of his own life, he had often struck swiftly during that long life, but also always, always he had held something back, a danger, a distraction, an uncertainty behind the line.

So – where was the piece she was holding back? And who was the opponent she was causing to hesitate – whom she would move past swiftly at the end? Certainly it was not Philippe, whom she would never outwit in this life, nor in any case had any desire to. Nor, clearly, was it the food writer Christopher Hare, whose mind was too confused to make him an adversary. Clearly, the enemy today had been her husband Abdul Yassou, simply, and this was what she had to keep clear in her own mind. Abdul Yassou, now, here. It was Abdul Yassou and his like that she was engaged with, to make an example of, for the benefit of those who might also consider a profitable career at the expense of others who ate only the meagre charity of Gaza. So it might be that the food writer immobilised in the room upstairs was the piece she kept back in this game, to be a nuisance and a distraction to the real adversary, which after all she and Philippe had in common.

But, yes, that still left the problem of Antun the maître d', who by now might be making his way home to an apartment that suddenly seemed to have walls of glass incapable of concealing him from either the French police or, what was worse, from the associates of Abdul Yassou, whose intelligence would be better than that of the police.

So, whatever happened, whatever her move, it would have to take care also of Antun and his nerves. Her cleaning-up of this mess would have to be as thorough as she could hear Philippe's had been upstairs where, even now, the food writer might be beginning to ask fate why he had chosen to act in that way.

There was another day she commemorated in the secrecy of her own memory, not as a performance like her grandmother's, nor like the pedagogic example of al-Hakim's backgammon moves, but as an instruction to her own instinct to act. How to move into the danger of a given situation? How to confront it, and how to pass through it? On that day in April 1970 when she was only eleven years old, the schools were closed because Fatah militias had stormed the American Embassy and then moved on to the US Information Service on Jebel Amman. Her father came rushing home shouting from his clinic with a smell of spilled mouthwash on him. Perhaps now it is starting, he was cursing – those fools, those children, did they think that Hussein and his camel-herding cronies would allow this to continue? Yes, they would see, he was right, now it began again, then it was the Jews and now it would be the camel-herding Bedouin that would oppress the Palestinians! And to think that he had welcomed that loud-mouthed Godless fool his cousin al-Hakim to be a guest in his house, worse fool that he was, now see if they were not marked for the attention of those camels! Yes, look, soon they would arrive!

But towards lunch time he calmed down and, insisting that even the *fedayeen* would be resting at this time from their labours of firing ammunition into the empty sky, in the heat of noon, as the radio also suggested they were, he sent her older brother Habib to accompany her on the bus to Jebel Amman for her English class at the British Council. Where, at once, when they stepped from the bus, they saw that the *fedayeen* were not resting after all, but were about to burn down the American Library nearby. Many were boys no older than her brother, they hardly looked strong enough to hold the Kalashnikovs they were carrying. When they saw her brother Habib in his respectable pants and jacket, some of them began to jeer because they were full of the bravado of the moment, and she felt him hesitate where he held her by the elbow at the side of the road across the traffic island opposite the British Council. The others from the bus had all rapidly dispersed away from the American Library, and away from the youths with their guns who were shouting there and in the streets and alleys they had blockaded in the vicinity of the First Circle traffic island. But now the only way to the British Council was through the rear entrance, which was in the opposite direction to that taken by the fleeing bus passengers.

When she felt her brother's hesitation and saw the laughter and excitement showing in the faces of the young *fedayeen* who were even then advancing towards them in a mob, shouting, from the narrow street beside the British Council, she felt her body and her mind make a decision together, in perfect unison. And as one of the boys lifted his Kalashnikov to fire exuberantly into the air over their heads, she seized her hesitating brother's arm and rushed with him directly into the faces of the advancing *fedayeen* – who then parted as though the eleven-year-old girl and her big brother were pushing the prow of a ship ahead of them through a strong current. They rushed directly through the column of youths, parting them, so close that she could smell the sweat and cigarettes of their day-long excitement and effort. And then they were through and out the other side. There were Bedouin police with an armoured car guarding the back entrance of the British Council, who opened the door in the great steel gate there and let her and Habib in. They hurried to the the roof of the British Council building, and she heard a loud cry go up in the street as the American director of the library arrived and was allowed to visit the building to see to the safety of the people there – but the *fedayeen* had already taken care to remove them, and soon those watching heard the sound, like heavy rolls of carpet dropped from balconies into the street, of bombs exploding in the library's elevator-shaft, and then the phosphorus explosives going off and white smoke gushing suddenly from the windows. The dull sounds of the explosions echoed back and forth between the hills of the city, and a great cacophony of barking dogs began then and continued into the evening, as if, like the young *fedayeen*, they could not stop once they had started.

But all she could think of then, watching the spectacle of the burning library from the roof of the British Council, while Habib reasserted his authority by scolding her and complaining about her to the others on the roof, was the moment of her decision. She was calm on the roof while her brother trembled, and she saw that he had even wet himself a little during their run, though she never mentioned this to anyone. Nor did she talk about the moment to anyone, not even when her brother misrepresented her action to their father, when at last they got home again.

The city was very quiet, later – because, her father said, there was now a curfew with army checkpoints appearing suddenly at the major intersections, as if the camel-herding Husseini had all along been waiting for an excuse, which they had now, to drive the trouble-making Palestinians from the city.

She had carried the memory of her decision and of its subsequent calmness into her life as her secret, it had been at her disposal more than once over the years, and now forty years later she sought its clarity and simplicity again as Philippe came back into the room, drying his hands on a towel which he then threw with disgust on the floor by the door to the truck garage.

It was five years after the burning of the American Library that handsome Abdul Yassou was sent by his father away from the outbreak of war in Beirut, to reside with his old friend and colleague in Amman and to seek opportunities in the city from which the *fedayeen* had, indeed, been expelled by Hussein's Bedouin, and into which the grateful Americans were, indeed, pouring dollars. That was when she became aware that Abdul Yassou was looking at her, but carefully, while her grandmother performed the yearly ritual of the Lydda key. Another four years and he appeared again, a little thicker and more manly, looking at her still but with less circumspection now, where she was living in Paris at the apartment of her brother Habib and his family on the Boulevard de la Chapelle and attending classes at the Campus Universitaire de Jussieu, with her *keffiyeh*-wearing friends.

What had she done with her secret memory of decision and calm then, at that moment, when her life turned towards Abdul Yassou? Towards his dangerous smile that reminded her of a shark, a white chevron shape, a bite waiting? Perhaps, at that time, her secret memory had deceived her. But then, it was also true that he had wooed her with distinction and success, he had been her strong lover, her first one. And that at this time she had lived more completely in the present than at any other, and that this *present* had remained so for a long time afterwards, even after she had left him – until this very day, perhaps.

'So, you have decided.' This was a question from which Philippe had removed the sense of interrogation.

'I have until morning.'

The older man sighed and made a slight sideways inclination of his head, at once affirmative and sceptical. 'Then you must also know that Antun has been foolish enough to telephone again after he was forbidden to do so. His mind is agitated. Your friend the writer was seen to enter the taxi. Now the police believe that he must be with us.'

'You mean, one of us?'

'Yes, since he can hardly have kidnapped himself.'

She waited, letting the tension of Philippe's sarcasm dissipate. There seemed to be a kind of tumult around her that she would have to pass through – a palpitation in the atmosphere of the squalid room, as if the air pressure there had thickened and was pressing on her senses.

Philippe shrugged, as if to say, You may want to take this intelligence into consideration. But then he added, 'Don't worry – the SIM to which Antun called has now gone where your friend's dinner went, into the sewer. Next time it will be Antun himself in person who announces that famous assassin's location to all the world. That woman with the memorable hair.'

So, yes, he had thought about what she had said about the risk of Antun, while cleaning up the mess in the bathroom. So, until dawn, this was her decision to make. Their necessary unanimity extended to that point at least.

At that moment the driver Mahfouz came in stinking of spray paint and with reddened, furious eyes from the fumes. He jerked his head at the floor above and made a slicing gesture across his throat – but Philippe stopped him before he could speak.

'Go and sleep, my friend,' he said calmly. 'In the morning early you have to drive to Italy, not so far, but without incident.' He paused, keeping her also within the span of his attention and his gaze. 'Here, we have a final move to make, Doctor Habash and I. The piece held back.'

So – he had guessed something of her intention. But perhaps

not all of it. She picked up the key to the room upstairs, and the gun that was on the table under her discarded grey wig, and left the room without speaking.

CHAPTER 4

He'd been looking at the closed window forever and thinking how much he longed for a view, any view – but better still, one across a wide blue bay, or across some paddocks to hills and mountains in the distance. Even the view through a car's windscreen would do the job, going somewhere that was almost like a view because it was in the distance. The distance that was like the future, over there. To be going into the distant future over there, with TG, with Miss Pepper.

But now he was in here. And closing the shutters and then the window had been like a decision he couldn't, now, change his mind about. Besides, there wasn't much to look at, out the window – a little glimpse of the twinkling hills, not far away; there was a place up there that did a good octopus terrine, they used a fennel bulb in the stewing – but in any case he was alone. Christopher-where-the-fuck-are-you.

Collecting mushrooms in the paddocks up behind Nana Gobbo's place, early in the morning, looking back down at Tolaga Bay, that was a view! – the long finger of the old jetty poked into the side of the sea that went out all the way to the sun that was coming up out of it. Uncle Antonio's Parkercraft tearing down the river towards the messy white water at the sandbar, out to his cray pots at the Rocks. After they were cooked, Christopher got to scoop his finger in the creamy mustard inside the bodies, the best bit. You had to get the mushrooms early before the worms did, or before the sheep trod all over them. Nana fried them up with bacon; they even tasted black. *Providence. Provvidenza.* Food with a view. His nostalgia for the past and some weird hope for the future were folding together, emulsifying – the image of a *salsa verde* came to mind, fragrant, tantalising because he couldn't separate the flavours. Yes, he was trying to *taste* his feelings. Crazy. He made a bowl-wiping gesture with his finger and pressed it to his lips. Then he found himself wiping his eyes, from what emotion he wasn't sure.

When the woman from the taxi came back in, he saw at once that she had hardened somehow. Before, there had been something a little sarcastic, mocking, in her manner, but at least that was a sign there had been some kind of connection between them – or so he thought. And she'd see that he hadn't tried to jump out the window, or scream for help. Here he was. He was still here. He didn't have to be a problem, she'd said so herself. Maybe she'd had an idea about how he could be useful? Where to go next with this? Or not, in which case, why couldn't he just walk?

It was the hope for some view of the future – a distinct taste – that made him smile at her. But she seemed only to flinch, coldly.

'So, you see, Mr Christopher Hare or "Rosenstein" whichever you prefer, it is easy to find you in the times of Google and also the name you like to hide in, yes? We Google you and *voilà*, a famous man, and also his, how do you say, "secret identity".' Her scorn made him gape; he felt his smile fall open, stupidly. 'How long did that take – long enough for you to think about your bizarre situation, I hope?' She sat down opposite him – her long hands, without gloves, now, hung down over her knees. Her nails were trimmed, and she wasn't wearing rings of any sort. He was staring at her in astonishment. Of course the longish grey hair had been a wig. Her real hair was cut short – it was dark and curly with little flecks of grey. She'd applied dark-coloured lipstick and some kind of neutral face-powder, and the overall effect was minimal and efficient. 'Also on the blogs people are asking, "Where is Thé Glacé?"' She pronounced 'blogs' as if with an umlaut, pushing her aubergine-coloured lips forward. 'They are missing her, this Thé Glacé, your broken-heart readers about food.' She leaned close and he caught a whiff of food on her breath, something with thyme. 'This Thé Glacé, maybe she is missing you also?' Her eyebrows were raised. 'Or maybe not?'

'Water,' he shouted, jumping to his feet. He felt an absurd, overwhelming disappointment. This wasn't what he'd expected. What use was the past, now? His tongue was sticking to the inside of his mouth. The woman also stood quickly and moved away, but not far. 'I need to drink some water. I already told you this. And it's none of your business. Thé Glacé, I mean. Or those stupid fucking bloggers. You leave her out of this.' He was ashamed of the moisture in his eyes, which he thought she would see as tears.

The thickset older man with the moustache had put his head around the door when Christopher shouted. The woman made her stopping gesture towards him, palm extended. She said a word, it sounded like 'Maya'.

'Tell me about this interesting *pen name*.' She accentuated the two letters 'n', making a mocking space between the words. She remained standing, facing him. 'This *Rosenstein*.' The nostrils of her bony, curved nose tightened with derision or perhaps amusement.

She was as tall as him, though her heels gave her an advantage. They were standing quite close together – he could smell the thyme on her breath. But he wouldn't step back. Now he was really angry – completely furious.

'Oh, please!' he shouted. 'Give me a break. Don't tell me. Let me guess.'

Her eyebrows went up again. 'It's Jewish?'

'He was a fucking Austrian,' he yelled. 'How should I

know if he was a Jew? He was a scientist. He lived a long time ago. A *histologist*!' He paused to wipe his mouth, and the tears from his eyes. He could hardly talk around the sticky dryness in his mouth. 'You know what that is?' he asked her, hearing the querulous tone in his voice – '*His-tol-o-gist*?' He was trying to mock her sarcasm with the pronunciation of 'pen-n-name', but it didn't come out right.

'He study tissue structures,' said the woman, with a deadpan expression. 'Am I right, *Mr Rosenstein*?' She seemed to be deciding whether to be offended or not. He was astonished and it must have showed in his face.

She shrugged. 'I am a doctor, usually I don't shoot people, but I can. I know how to do it. I can do it very well. But usually I try to make them better. Not always doing it, but we try.' She reached out a bony hand and pushed him quite gently towards an armchair. Behind her, the bulky older man came in holding a glass of water, his little finger delicately extended.

A doctor! – what next? She handed him the glass. 'Have a drink of water, Mr Hare. I think we call you this, it's better, otherwise you get upset. And we try, yes? To make something useful? Because I don't want to shoot you. That's not really what I prefer to do in my life. Making people better, more like cooking than killing I think. Maybe we have something in common, Mr Hare. Anyway, we can try.' But her manner was still hard, and he sensed that she had prepared herself.

But try what? What could they try? No longer moody and sarcastic, the woman with short salt-and-pepper hair now seemed to be all will and determination, and he sensed that there were absolute limits to her patience. She had a deadline. Perhaps he was her deadline? The thought was obvious, yet it filled him with a kind of familiar inertia. Deadlines – a lifetime of them!

'Listen,' he said, 'that *pen-n-name*.' Now, he could even tell himself the truth. 'I used to use it. When I needed to . . .'

'. . . to protect yourself. Your *métier.*' A faint smile lifted the corners of the doctor's hard mouth. She waved one hand dismissively. 'It's all right. We all do it, Mr Hare. But I do not think you are a coward.' That chesty bark of her laugh. 'And in any case, not so successful, your secret identity.' Then her moment of humour was over; her expression hardened.

A faint chemical smell had entered the room, and he saw her notice that he'd sniffed it – but she kept her impassive look and her silence. She was waiting for him to make the next move, ask the next question, set something in motion. But he didn't have any power in this situation as far as he could see and, anyway, he was exhausted. The excitement of his sprint down the stairs and into the taxi, even the involuntary bravado of his hoarse vomit in the lavatory, closing the shutters – these stimuli had drained away.

'Actually, I'm really tired,' he said, and though he tried to stop it, an enormous yawn prised his jaws apart and made his eyes squeeze shut and water.

Her slap, which he didn't see coming because of the yawn, snapped his head around. 'And what, this is a hotel, Mr Hare?' She was standing over him, close. If he could get up quickly he could rush her – but of course he couldn't. He wouldn't. 'And that was a *taxi*?' She took one of her long strides away from him. Then he saw that she had the gun in one hand – she must have taken it from her jacket pocket. He couldn't help it, he didn't make them do it, but his hands flew up in front of him to make a shield.

'No, please, I'm sorry.'

'*Sorry*?' Her scorn was also incredulous.

'And it was, after all. A taxi.'

Her huff of frustration, her head-wag – had they reached another moment when something was going to change?

'And I've stayed in worse hotels.' He waited for a moment. 'May I ask your name?'

The woman folded herself carefully into the armchair

opposite him and placed the gun on her side of the table.

'In another situation, Mr Hare, in a nice hotel perhaps, sharing a taxi, we are perhaps at a convention about food, what to do about the problem of it, a famous food writer has some interesting suggestions perhaps, we can discuss how things are in the refugee camps, in Baqa'a, or shall we say Gaza as a whole, nutrition, the *menu*, Mr Hare . . . yes, in another situation we are having perhaps an agreeable conversation, an enjoyable one probably, and in these circumstances when you tell me how *sorry* you are I have another opinion of it, not a lot better, we can't be sure of that, but anyway different. Different from this situation, Mr Hare, where you are now and where I am also, in this room.'

This was the first time he'd heard her speak at any length and he was completely floored by it. She'd spoken with a kind of control that resembled precise biting.

'May I say too, Mr Hare, that in more . . .' – she paused, thinking – '. . . *genial* circumstances I, too, might enjoy what is your evident sense of humour. But,' she tapped the gun that lay on the table, 'as we both know, this is not a hotel and that was not a taxi. And this,' tapping the gun, 'is not an aeroplane ticket or a nice piece of chicken or . . .' She waved her hand impatiently in his face. 'You have to wake up, Mr Hare. Wake up! And no, I am not going to tell you how I am called.'

'What difference would it make, if you're going to shoot me?'

That surprised her – and the tone of his own voice surprised him as well. Had he 'woken up' as she'd demanded? Nothing had really changed; he was still sitting hunched up in the armchair where her slap had driven him back, she was still sitting forward in her chair opposite him, one hand close to the gun on the table between them, and the acrid whiff of what smelled like paint was still, inexplicably, wafting into the room at something after midnight. It was breezy outside

– the jalousie shutters rattled from time to time on the other side of the glass. The rest of the house was silent, so perhaps the men were sleeping.

There was a place high in his guts, just under where his ribs parted and above where his stomach, these days, rested on top of his pants, where he was used to feeling the effects of eating too much of some things, for example rich Provençal rabbit cooked in red wine with thyme and juniper. But now a placid sensation seemed to have developed where he might rather have expected a dyspeptic burn. It was a soft sensation, calm, and it seemed to spread out to his breathing. Weights dropped from his shoulders – his shoulders themselves drooped, as though no longer resisting some pressure or other. His thighs stopped trembling and he let his hands hang down the sides of the armchair. No, he wasn't afraid. He didn't know what he was. But at least he was calm.

The woman saw this, or something. She seemed to be trying to encourage him with her silence. *Yes, yes, this is better. Keep going!*

'That's true, isn't it?' he asked her. 'If you tell me your name that means you're going to shoot me. And if you don't . . . ? Tell me your name, I mean?'

She continued to watch him, not speaking, without expression.

'Am I right?'

'My name is Maya Yazbeck.' Her smile shocked him – at once savage and amused. She hummed a harsh little tune, beating time with a long index finger. 'I am a popular carabet singer.' Then shaking her head, the smile gone – a vicious, impatient tut-tut with her tongue. 'You believe that, *Mr Rosenstein*?

But this had to be the moment. He pushed his new calmness towards her scorn.

'I'm serious.' He meant it. He believed it. 'These camps that you . . . that's why you . . . ?

'That's why I *did it*? You think?' Then she was tired of this. 'But you know nothing, I think.'

'But maybe I can . . . ?'

'Maybe you can *learn*?'

'Maybe I can help?'

'My name is Dr Hawwa Habash,' said the woman, in a flat, factual tone of voice, as if merely repeating a bureaucratic requirement. 'I am a physician and my speciality is *pédiatrique*. I look after children.' Then she smiled her not-smile. 'I am not your teacher, Mr Hare. Or your future. And now you are convinced that I am going to shoot you. Of course this is possible.'

Was she watching for his response? Was this a threat? The calm sensation in his midriff continued to spread, reassuringly – it seemed to need oxygen, and he heaved a deep sigh, not of emotion but out of comfortable physical necessity, as if the event that was taking place in his stomach had expanded and created a space that needed to be filled with ordinary air, a space of *now*.

His companion in the room seemed to misinterpret this sigh – she shook her head as if disappointed – but then, how could she know what he was feeling? The sensation was unfamiliar even to him.

'Yes, you may sigh, as if it is your fate for which I have now written the *ordonnance*. But let me tell you, Mr Hare, that the world of my colleagues in this house is indeed a simple one. In this it resembles yours. As you have described it to me, just a little. Your,' that thinking pause again, '*analytic*, I think you say in English.'

'Analysis,' he said. 'My analysis.' And then he thought, Why not? 'Not something I'm often credited with.' She was waiting for him to shut up. 'Apart from food, that is.' He made a sewing-up motion across his lips, to show good faith.

The woman smiled at this, but without much humour. 'But you see, I have not shoot you, or had the others take you somewhere and do it, so perhaps it is not so simple, or perhaps it does not need to be so simple.'

'Dr Hawwa Habash,' he said, 'who works with children.' He remembered the place names she'd spoken – he knew one of them. 'In Gaza,' he added.

'So, I can see, you like to take risks. First you jump in the taxi and now you expose yourself to my information, you begin my interrogation. Why is that, I wonder?' She waited, keeping her gaze directly in his face. Expecting an answer. 'Perhaps it is because you want to die, Mr Hare. You think I will oblige, as you saw in the restaurant?'

She seemed to be joking, but he surprised himself with the certainty and confidence of his answer. 'No,' he murmured, feeling the thought reach urgently ahead of what he was saying. 'I don't want to die. I want to live. Believe me, shit, do I ever.'

'And this is why you jump in the taxi and now interrogate me, knowing now my name, about where I do my work, with this weapon here that you have seen I can use?' She was pinching the bag under one eye again, rolling it between her long fingers. When she let go of it the skin remained raised, a little reddened, before subsiding back to being a plain mark of weariness.

His first response was a simple *Yes – yes!* But the illogic of it – or the shock of the thought's strangeness – stopped him. He realised that his mouth was dumbly open. It was as though he kept catching glimpses of himself as she was seeing him.

'You look tired,' he said. 'Perhaps you should get some rest.'

Her look of annoyance struck him as ungrateful. But then, inexplicably, she began to laugh – real laughter, not that clanging bark of derision he'd become used to hearing. Her large mouth opened wide, she fanned herself with one hand, and the harsh sound of her laughter almost seemed to rattle her bony frame. She even smacked herself on the thigh – the woman who'd slapped his face, hard, only moments ago. Her unrestrained guffaws conveyed powerful physical confidence, and he felt his own compliant response shaping a hopeful grin, then a titter. But he didn't know what was so funny. And then, again, that abrupt shift, scaring the living daylights out of him. Her laughter stopped when her hand stopped smacking her thigh and instead smacked violently down on the table. Once, twice. The dirty cups and the Coke bottle rattled. Then she shook her big clenched fist, with her index finger extended, in his face, right under his nose.

'Why – did – you – do – it!' She spat the word 'it' with such rage that a little froth stuck to her bottom lip. Though she'd startled him for a moment, he still felt weirdly calm.

'I seem to remember asking you the same question not so long ago – Dr Habash. And does my life depend on the answer?' How prissy he sounded – TG would have had a field day. *Oh, Chris-tuh-for!*

'To what the answer – why did I do what I did, or why did you do it?' Her chest was still heaving a little with the force of her breath, and the nostrils of her large nose were pinched and pale with fury, or restraint.

'Whichever you like.' How strange, to feel so calm, when really what he wanted to ask was, What are you waiting for? Why don't you just shoot me now and get it over with? Because she seemed to be playing with him, in some way he couldn't figure out. She was shaking her head from side to side in disbelief, tut-tutting.

'So, okay, why did you?' He easily resisted saying, Show me yours, I'll show you mine – but the fact that the thought even occurred to him made him smile again. But then he quickly shut the smile down – no more yelling from scary Dr Habash, thank you very much! 'You tell me why you shot that man and . . .'

'And the woman also?'

'I was going to say, and then I'll try to explain why I ran after you – but yes, why did you shoot her?' Again, he easily stopped himself from blurting out the next thing that came into his head, which was the French phrase he knew, *crime passionel*. Because nothing about that romantic explanation fitted what he'd seen and what was highly organised in some way, the taxi, the house, the other older man with the moustache who seemed to be keeping an eye on things.

But then she beat him to it, anyway. '*Enfin*, this was not exactly what I believe you will be thinking, *un crime passionel*, how do you say that? – that is in any case quite banal.'

'That? Banal? Boy, I'd like to see what you guys do for kicks.'

Clearly, again, he'd nearly gone too far – or else she didn't really understand the joke, such as it was. He even felt a little exhilarated that he was having a conversation like this, with the woman who clearly wasn't joking when she said she might have to shoot him. Exhilarated but still calm – or able to be exhilarated because he was still calm. He'd felt the same way with his head in the fake Gucci bag, on the way here.

'You know what?' he said. 'I've just thought of something?' He had, too. It was Nana's rooster, back at Tolaga Bay. By day he'd strutted importantly, with little tosses of his inflamed comb, his shrewd eyes on the watch for misbehaving hens or young Christopher approaching with food scraps. But in the evening, after the last spasms of crazed yodelling that announced that his hens had roosted, Nana would plonk an empty cardboard box over him on the floor of the hen-house, and here, after a few muffled shrieks, he would become calm. He would time-out until Nana Gobbo took the box off again in the morning, once everybody was already awake and on the job.

Did he, Christopher, feel less calm, now, remembering the

stupid rooster under the box? No – rather, a line of memory seemed to have opened up that ran through his life and into the box of the present moment. The momentum seemed to want to continue, it seemed to be inevitable, somehow, to be going forward beyond this moment, and all he had to do was to accept the choices that appeared – to see the choices when they appeared and to accept the one that was moving his view forward.

Dr Hawwa Habash was waiting – for whatever it was he'd thought of. But he sat there for a moment, feeling around in his mind for the limits of this enclosure within which he felt so peaceful. Not bored, not impatient, not frightened, not harassed – not even missing TG any more, or only a bit. What was this about? And that line of simple memory that seemed now – now that he had his head in the bag or under the box, in this dirty room – seemed now to spool away like the view of a country road through the back window of a car. Back along through a terrible rowdy mess of years, flat-out or written-off, with yelling in kitchens or in beds, slamming doors, laughing and laughing, the sound of his suitcase wheels trundling along somewhere at night, the television studio floor-manager yanking his earphones off and throwing them on the floor, the lines of people who'd already eaten too much waiting to get their Christopher Hare-slash-Mary Pepper books signed so they could go home and fuck themselves up even more – that view along which he saw himself over and over saying *I'm sorry* on the one hand and on the other standing all puffed up across the table with Robuchon's famous *caille caramelisée avec une pomme purée à la truffe* on it, utter rubbish, he'd mocked it by making it into a rocket launch-pad with the quail pointing up from a foaming base of *purée*, and Robuchon's *chef de cuisine* in Monaco, Christophe Cussac, the almighty lieutenant, yelling at him from the other side of the table that if he published a *single word,* that magazine would be *pariah*, its name would be *shit*. And almost out of frame, lovely Miss Mary Pepper, whom they hadn't yet fought over calling 'Thé Glacé', let alone TG, grinning behind her elegant, 'wealthy Chelsea' hand.

Once again, the room's stale air rushed into that calm space inside him – not a sigh, though when he let it out again he allowed it to vibrate his lips, clownishly.

'Never mind, Doctor,' he said. 'It was just a thought.' What had also occurred to him was that it was only because he'd rushed down the restaurant stairs on impulse and jumped into the white taxi with this woman that he'd discovered his calm place, his rooster box, his time-out present moment, and this view from it back along the crazy path of his life.

The woman shrugged as if to say, What's wrong with thinking? Still she didn't speak. But then she picked the gun up from the table and dropped it into the side pocket of her jacket – withdrawing her hand afterwards, and folding it with the other in her lap. So that seemed to indicate something.

'Okay,' he said. 'This may sound crazy. But I think I'm here because this is the present. This is the only place from which I can go forward.' He tried to say 'go forward' with an ironic tone, but she didn't hear it. Her expression just waited. The large eyes lidded with weariness or thought. He tried hard to make what he was saying go past her watchfulness.

'Where I was before, in the restaurant, that was the past. I was stuck in it. When I ran after you, I escaped. I escaped from the past. From,' he couldn't help it, mocking himself to please her unexpected sympathy, 'from Rosenstein.'

Still no expression on her face, the long hands folded in her lap.

'Sorry,' he said – and heard himself. 'And sorry for the *sorry*. Probably that doesn't make any sense. What I just said.'

He wanted to try again with the future view, that vivid taste of hope. *Maybe I can help?* Why was that such a joke?

But he saw her lips hesitating over what to say.

'On the contrary,' murmured Hawwa Habash. 'It make very good sense, I understand completely. For me it is also perhaps not so different. What you say about the past.' Then he saw her pause and collect her thoughts, or the words for them. 'But there are some things I have to tell you, *Christopher.*'

It seemed to him that her pause had been about a decision to use his Christian name – to move herself into a space of some intimacy, to make herself vulnerable, even – this woman who had smacked him so hard across the side of the head that his ears were still ringing, who had held a revolver against his ribs and thrown his cellphone out the car window.

'Now you must listen carefully, because this future you see for yourself, it has conditions. I will explain. You have to understand, it is important.'

'Life and death.' And then he nearly said sorry again, at her grimace of annoyance.

'Yes, if you like. But not yours only. There is a danger now for us, from you. You are a danger. I will explain.' She seemed to be beginning again. 'But please – do not tell me that you are sorry. I can see that you like to do this. Now it is too late for your *sorry,*' – that thinking pause – 'Christopher.'

'Okay, Doctor.'

'And please – do not play with me. I am not your doctor, specifically I am not your *therapist.* And I do not think you are a child. My responsibility is . . .' But then she lifted her clenched hands impatiently, as if holding her anger back. 'I advise you, do not waste my time, or . . .'

Or.

Yes, the word entered his calm space in-the-bag, the box, the room, and settled there as if it, too, might start squawking once its cover was removed. Meanwhile he listened to her explain that this was indeed *une mission secrète*, that the cabaret singer's name, Maya Yazbeck, was indeed her *nom de cadre*, that the window table he'd occupied in the restaurant had been the one where the big man's bodyguard would have been seated had he been in the restaurant, watching the street – and that therefore he, Christopher, had been a signal. When, from the taxi, she first saw someone in the window, she had to make a decision. This was their chance. Much work had made it possible. So then, from the other side of the road, even though this made her more visible from the restaurant and increased her risk, she was able to look again at who was in the window – not the bodyguard of her target, she was then quite sure. So, did he understand, it was as though by being a signal involuntary he was already compromised in what was going to happen.

He saw again the silver-haired woman flick a glance up at his window from beneath the cover of her small red umbrella. He saw, earlier, the maître d' remove the *reservé* sign on the window table – '*M'sieur . . . pour vous . . . pas de problème . . . bon appétit . . .*'

'Do you understand?'

Oh yes, he was beginning to.

'So, then, after Antun indicate to me when I come in that the window seat is uncompromised . . .'

'Antun?'

'He is the maître d' of that restaurant. He arrange some things for us. Soon I have to explain some more about him. But listen.'

The man's imploring gesture as he, Christopher Hare, galloped towards the stairs throwing his table-napkin to the floor – the solitary diner whom the man didn't even know as the famous food and restaurant critic, even though he'd removed the reserved sign from the table just as Christopher Hare had come to expect over the years. Yes, that had seemed odd at the time.

'So, at that moment, Antun is thinking, who is this man? Maybe he, Antun, make a mistake? So, to protect himself, he cannot stop you – or he do not know how to act? What are you, a police? So he is very confused and also afraid. Afraid he make a mistake, afraid the police think he is involved. And then, the police tell him that somebody else see you jump in the taxi. So, of course . . .'

Or.

He concentrated on watching her expression while she spoke. She was trying really hard to be clear and simple. It mattered to her that he understood. Understood what? The direction of his future. She was explaining that because the police now believed he was involved in the murder – he had, after all, run down the stairs with her bag and jumped into the taxi – he was now in the position of being an unreliable member of their – she struggled for the word – '. . . *équipe, cadre, vous comprenez?*'

Yes, he understood.

. . . and that as a consequence, being unreliable, he was a great danger to them at this time. And therefore.

He understood.

. . . and also, that Antun would now require a solution to this problem of unreliability. Because now the police were looking at him, Antun, also, with a certain interest. To answer some questions that he could not, with ease. Did he understand?

Yes, that he also understood.

And now he felt a little sick – was he tired? Or was it because of his fear coming towards him from the future? From the future moment when his protection would be lifted, like the box off Nana Gobbo's tranquil rooster?

She was looking at him with that expression at once impassive and demanding – one he'd begun to know well. He sensed a concealed urgency in her. Which of course was about him, as a deadline. He felt the familiar word, his old foe, fall into two parts in his mind. Dead line.

'You have a deadline, of course?'

Her flinch was minimal. '*Dead line?*' Her pronunciation of the unfamiliar word separated it, just as his thought had, but she concealed her alarm with a frown.

'Yes.' He fumbled for the French word. '*Un délai, une date limite*. I think I'm it, aren't I? Where the buck stops? I mean, obviously.'

'In the morning, quite early, we have to go.' That was all she was going to say. But there was something else going on there, in that tired, haughty face, that he couldn't get the hang of.

'So,' she said, shrugging again, 'an impasse.'

There was no point letting the 'dead line' thought inside the perimeter of his calm, but there it was. Along with a kind of nausea.

'What do you want me to do?' He risked pointing at her. 'And you haven't told me your side of the story. Like you promised.' Her impassive look. 'Why you did it.'

'I suggest you occupy yourself a little time with some thoughts about your situation, as I have explain it. Maybe some people you like to contact. Maybe this Thé Glacé. Who is your wife, I think. I can arrange for you a contact.'

No more *Christopher* he noticed. Well, that was short-lived. She stood up carefully, with her gun hand in her jacket pocket, as if she half expected him to make a move of some kind.

'Where are you going?'

That little smile, a tightening of her cheeks, without humour. 'It is very charming, under the circumstances, to discuss philosophy with such a famous *food writer*.' She was still angry, after all. 'Unfortunately I have some preparations. Please, think what you would like.'

What would I like?

Then, in that smoothly striding way, she crossed the room and went out. He heard the key turn in the lock.

Would he like to contact TG? What about Bob? What

would he say? 'Help – I've succeeded in kidnapping myself?' This was, after all, his last assignment for Bob – his last trip, his swan song.

It's been marvellous, Chris. Bloody marvellous. I can't thank you enough.

No, what would Bob really say? 'Well, I hope you can raise your own ransom.' Very funny, Bob, but what would you care? 'It's a tough old world, Chris, and you've had a damned good run.'

There was the mineral water moment. Nasty chilly February day, he went into the Thurloe Place office knowing something or other was up, and Bob had two bottles of water on his desk.

'Tell me, Chris, what's the difference?' No time wasted.

'Come off it Bob, don't piss me around.'

'How's Mary?'

'How should I know?' So much for the pleasantries.

Then Bob's patronising fucking little talk. The industry had crossed a line. A 'Rubicon'. On one side magazine sales were down, on the other some were holding or going up. But it was tough all round. On the downside were, so to speak, specialist mineral water *sommeliers*, if they could be dignified with the term; on the up was tap water. On the up was traditional but not with duck fat. The Prince of Wales's organic eggs, Chris, for God's sake – Waitrose supermarkets had a special Royal Organic section, hadn't he noticed – from The Estates? Farmers' markets, your grandmother's handwritten recipe for piccalilli, those wizened ex-models growing their own Swiss chard in window boxes, Fair Trade coffee and, of course, all that 100% Pure nonsense from, where was it again, Chris? Middle Earth? Even, God help us, reminders of frugal household hints from World War Two. How to make your own *soap*, Chris, from lard. Mid-to-low range Spanish and Chilean wines, you wouldn't believe the rubbish that was being written about them. Jamie Oliver's school lunches. Explore your region, Chris, your suburb – Camberwell was it? Plenty of ethnic stuff over there, jerk pork – no, come to think of it, too fatty.

'And the downside, Bob?' He was trying to keep his temper.

The thing was, it was a tap-water market these days. They'd had to re-think the look-and-feel of the graphics, take that glisten off the images: too much resemblance to well lubricated sexual organs, Chris. 'Gastro porn' was the ridiculous tut-tut term being bandied about. But it was true, the big money advertisers were going underground. Their cheese people, their seasoned-game suppliers, their importers of *andouillette*. The chic readers wanted photographs of lettuce and bleached khaki shorts. Preferably lettuce *in* bleached khaki shorts, ha ha, Chris.

'And, Bob, your point?'

There were two points. One was that gusto was *passé*, especially when the colourful food being eaten with gusto was in exotic but impoverished places where the wistful faces of starving children kept haunting the copy.

'You know what I'm talking about, Chris.'

He did, as a matter of fact. TG's photographs. He also knew what the next bit was going to be about.

Sure enough.

The second point was that Christopher's magic was part of a double act and that, of course, wasn't happening any more, as Bob hardly needed to remind him. No one was sadder about that than Bob, but what was he expected to do? He'd made the silly girl his project for long enough, and then look what she did.

'Sorry, Chris, just not the same without Mary, with all due respect, and on top of that our readers are telling us that you are past your use-by.'

'I'm forty-five, Bob, you prick. I made you rich.'

'You could have made yourself rich, too, if you hadn't

stuffed handfuls of it down the toilets of the exotic food Meccas with which your brand is now associated, so don't get high-and-mighty with me, Chris, after all . . .'

Yes, yes, *after all* it was he, Bob, who'd given Christopher his break a decade ago, don't forget it, and – violins – 'It's a tough old world, Chris, and you've had a damned good run.'

The water in the glass on the table in front of him, among the dirty cups and the empty Coke bottle and cigarette butts, was certainly mineral water, but the situation didn't feel too fucking much like the new brand with the sexy shine taken off the lithe, entwined *pappardelle*, TG's pale limbs glazed in sunlight on the bed last time he saw them, neither of them spring chickens any more, but all the same.

'Come on, Bob. I'm on my arse. One last run.'

So – here he was. He sipped slightly fizzy water from the heavy glass. Thank Christ the people in the house hadn't been subjected to Bob's pious lecture and given him tap water to drink, or he'd be trying to get his arse over the hole in the floor across the landing any time now.

He eased the image of TG's languid, pasta-pale limbs from his mind. For some time now the image had always come with the same caption: *Not much use to you if you can't eat it or fuck it, isn't that so, Christopher?*

Always *Christopher*, even after ten years. *Chris-to-pher.*

But what did she expect him to say? Every single image in her now-famous exhibition was like a kick in the nuts. The great slag-heaps of wet, cascading food collaged from places where the two of them had hooked little fingers over the table and coo-cooed like doves; the huge, purple, bulging arses cunts and breasts made out of piled aubergines they'd probably enjoyed together in a simple *aubergines à la lyonnaise*. Worst of all, the ultimate betrayal, the gross forest of erect pricks with impaled fleshy mushroom flanges sticking up out of the mess of what must have been a *Cappon*

Magro. Now it looked like a pile of vomit, intact scampi peering out of it with black, beady eyes on stalks.

'But the *Cappon*, TG? For the love of God.'

'What about it?'

'That was when we . . .'

'No, Christopher, if you remember, that was when *you*. It was usually when *you*. Invariably.'

'No, it was when *we*. That was the night we decided to get married. In case you've forgotten. That night with the *Cappon*. In Genoa. Christ, TG, you could have warned me. I had no idea. How can we work after this?'

'Well, perhaps we can't, Chris-to-pher.'

She had the knack of making him feel like a hick, just by the way she stood. A kind of weariness in the shoulders, one slinky hip stuck out. After all these years. There was a buzzing and squawking of comment and conversation in the gallery, and excited faces kept inserting themselves into his view of TG, over her shoulder or from the side, apologetic but keen, grinning, wide-eyed – but then retiring because they could see that she was having a bit of a tiff. Wasn't that her husband, the *food writer*?

'Not much use to you if you can't eat it or fuck it, isn't that so, Christopher?'

'What on earth are you talking about?'

'Oh for God's sake, does it always have to be about *you*?'

You'd have had to be really close to hear her, she had the knack of spitting the words through her teeth, with a kind of precision, straight into him, but it felt to him – it felt as if she might as well have been yelling at the top of her voice to the whole gallery-full of people, over the chatter, the rattling glasses, the music that was playing, something Cuban.

'But you never told me what you were doing, TG.'

'And why the fuck should I have, Christopher? Gosh, I wonder what you'd have said then? *Please don't do this to me, TG*.' Her mimicry was spot on – even the pout. 'This is *my* exhibition, Christopher, it's my gig, I've waited twenty years for this, I spent the first ten trotting in and out of rehab and the next ten being your Thé Glacé. Well, it's not about you, it's not about *us*. Why can't you let me have it? Try saying, *Congratulations, sweetheart, well done darling, bloody marvellous. What a surprise!*'

He knew her well enough to see the tears lurking back in there somewhere, but when he began to shape the words 'I'm sorry' and reach out a hand towards her, she just hissed, 'Fuck off, Christopher. Just leave me alone. Just . . .'

Probably, they could have patched it up. But probably not. The exhibition reviews were incredible; TG was doing interviews for the same colour sections and lifestyle fold-outs that were putting Bob's gastro-porn magazine out of business; she was being blogged by both Charlotte Higgins and Jonathan Jones in the *Guardian*, she got into *Flux* magazine, there was a live interview on Radio 4. Then their flat began to get calls in Italian, French and Asian accents. She got a dealer in New York and another in Berlin. Her London dealer talked past him and never once asked about his work. Not once. Quite a lot of the reviews hinted archly that she'd had 'a long apprenticeship' – photographs of her had that recovered-junkie look. Some of these mentioned her twenty-year career as a 'food photographer' and depicted her as an elegant anorexic. Most of these made humorous references to her husband, 'the well-known food writer, Christopher Hare'. Christ almighty, she ate like a horse! Hoeing into that *Cappon Magro*!

And who the hell was Christopher Hare? The dope didn't really exist anymore – let alone his pathetic understudy, Rosenstein! Hare was back in the mediocre restaurant in the off-season where the maître d' called Antun had planted him in the window table reserved for some goon who didn't show up, which was why Dr Habash had crossed the road and shot the fat guy and the tarty-looking woman. Rosenstein might as well still be there, too, for that matter, like some kind of shop-window mannequin. In fact, he was. He was *there*.

Was this what he'd always done? Leave himself behind? He, Christopher Hare, even seemed to have walked out on, run out on, his Maori uncles and cousins with Italian names up there on the Coast in the 'Bay of Plenty'. 'Plenty of what? – Plenty of bloody Eyeties!' was how the joke used to run around Nana Gobbo's table when he was a kid. And 'Hare'? The man who gave him that name was unknown to him, and just as well, according to his mother. She took her Italian mother's maiden name when Hare shot through. Mietta Gobbo was in the ground not far from Nana Gobbo in the graveyard with a sea view; Mietta went there first. All he remembered was the lovely down on her cheeks, like a peach – his little-boy lips pouted to brush back and forth across that tiny tickle. Now the people who loved him were gone, or he'd left them. In his heart he knew that the people he thought of as 'friends' were more interested in getting good reviews than in him – they might as well have been interested in that ventriloquist's dummy, 'Rosenstein'.

What would I like?

He didn't have a clue. What was the point of wanting anything? Really, all he wanted was to be here, in this dull, smelly room, inside the rooster-box of the present, waiting for the moment when someone would lift the cover off to let the sunshine in. But that was crazy.

It was crazy thinking Dr Habash might release him. But he couldn't help it – he could taste his own hope, feel the shape of his crowing.

Just for a moment, he saw himself as Dr Habash might – his lips pushed forward in a silent 'doodle-doo', the uncontrollable tears making his eyes glisten appealingly.

CHAPTER 5

Food is love, food is love, food is love!

She could picture herself with her hands over her ears, going 'La la la la la la!' Not hearing you, Christopher.

In her empty flat.

With the memories. And turning up the same old music.

Next after the beef cheeks at Le Baratin was Franck Cerutti's stewed salt cod at Alain Ducasse's Le Louis XV in Monaco. Sounded utterly vile, the cod anyway.

'You'll love it!'

And she did. Absolutely. Adored. It. Another *food is love* moment. She even didn't mind when Christopher reached over like a greedy lout and stole a forkful of the stockfish tripe from her plate. He was in heaven. Contagious-bliss heaven.

'Brilliant, brilliant!'

Maybe it was the lemon sauce.

No, she knew what it was. By now.

She fought off his fork when it came back a second time. They were children having a sword fight. Even the reproving waiters were smiling.

She knew by now what it was with Christopher: a disarming magic, a transformation. A performance he could do, between naiveté and a confidence trick. It was both attractive and frightening.

Somewhere in the vicinity of the cigarette-smelly, clanking lift from the grubby first-floor residential next to the Opéra in Nice and the white and gold luxury of the Hôtel de Paris in Monte Carlo, on the train they'd walked back across Nice to catch, or on the walk from the gusty station in Monaco, he transformed. He assumed this confidence. He brought it out, sulkily, like a costume, then he put it on.

And then he grinned. Shameless. Ready for anything.

This bully-boy Christopher challenged you to doubt him, the act of himself, to puncture his confidence, but nobody did. Like a classic confidence trickster, everything on the cheap, and then – ba-boum! His crumpled suit, his mop of hair, his travel-weariness after the TGV from Paris and too much wine with the beef cheeks at Le Baratin – transformed. Careless, confident, not stylish, but what was the word?

Undeniable.

His undeniable grin, looking up at the dreadful Rococo tondo of a naked Aurora amongst dawn-flushed clouds and tumbling cherubs in the ceiling of the restaurant.

'Elle nous regarde, la rousse là.' His undeniably couldn't-care-less French.

'Bien sûr, la belle espionne de Monsieur Ducasse!' The sommelier poured for Christopher to taste. 'On ne peut jamais être trop prudent!'

'Il a des couilles, n'est-ce-pas, le patron.' Christopher vulgarly weighed the imaginary Ducasse bollocks in both hands, grinning at the sommelier. Undeniably fishing.

But already the man had this rumpled foreigner with the bad accent down as *undeniable.* A room full of people who creaked, they were so proper, so *prudent*, so well turned-out, not to mention so filthy rich. But Christopher left them for dead.

Christopher with the magazine's business card hidden in his wallet. His new trump card, saving it.

The sommelier filled her glass with a saucy flourish and a complimenting nod to Christopher.

'See? It's you, Mary Pepper.' That big louche grin. 'That

certain something. You've got them wondering. Who is this perfect pale flute of *grand cru*?'

'Oh, for God's sake, Christopher. Don't be such a pretentious twat.'

But it wasn't her. It was undeniably him. Even though he didn't tell the maître d' about the magazine until they'd finished and he'd paid, slipping Bob's business card into the embossed *addition* wallet along with a generous tip. And then making a mockingly self-deprecating show of their departure.

'Can't let them know we're catching the train back to the slums, Pepper.' Terribly pleased with himself.

Or, perhaps, it was them. The two of them.

This was a thought she tried out carefully. Began to try out.

It was a little chilly when they left the restaurant. He put his floppy horse-smelly jacket around her shoulders as they walked to the station.

'Got to keep Miss Pepper hot.'

Was that flirting? Undeniably. Stupid, but yes.

Was she flattered? Hardly – but a little bit of excitement was beginning to build up. She knew what was going on, they'd probably end up in bed together before the trip was over. Probably shouldn't. Definitely shouldn't. Probably would.

It had been a long time since she'd enjoyed flirting with herself, for that matter. Teasing herself with her own hesitation. She didn't kiss him goodnight in the dingy hotel corridor. In the pit of her stomach she knew what would happen if she did.

But also that hint of mockery in his confidence. Which was compelling but repellent.

In the little bathroom mirror she saw the half-smiling waif she knew, a loose lock of pale hair making her blink and shake her head – yes, no?

The next day they went back to Le Louis XV. She took photographs of the empty dining room once the dinner settings had been laid – but with guests, *jamais*! Nev-er!

She made an art-school joke – 'Nev-er in Nevers!' – but Christopher didn't get it. He gave her a blank look. He was drinking an apéritif with Cerutti and making notes.

Then they were more or less dismissed. Yes, she'd noticed. There she'd been, photographing the table-settings and the décor again, *plus ça change*. That was a bit gloomy.

They went and drank a bottle of wine down by the marina. She saw his mood change. The night before he'd been an *undeniable* guest in the restaurant, impervious and confident. But the next day, back in the same place, he was just another food writer doing his job, and it was just Cerutti's job to give him a little time.

And later that day, at dinner, he made a complete arse of himself, 'doing a competitive comparative' in Monaco again, but at Robuchon's Métropole Palace this time. Too much to drink before dinner, couldn't find his confidence costume, got dreadfully sullen and defensive, failed to charm the sommelier, blew his food writer cover early, built a silly Voyager spaceship with his quail, had a vulgar screaming match with Cussac, was lucky not to get them thrown out.

Oh yes, amusing up to a point, she even enjoyed it. But that night he wasn't *undeniable*, he was mostly just a boor and a bore. And there was no nice roomy coat around her shoulders while he sulked all the way back to Nice on the uncomfortable train.

He didn't flirt, either. Not even one of those moist, winning looks. Sulk, sulk, sulk all the way to the grimy lift, and straight to his room. Boring.

But then, the sleeper to Venice.

But now, what was she expected to do with all this stuff? The memories that piled up, like the shambles of an after-dinner Christopher kitchen. Scraps, spills, discards, corks.

Also the hangover, the gossip, the flirtations, the bad moods.

But the *undeniables*.

But now, the nostalgia tracks. Graham Parker, *You try to reach a vital part of me*.

Three in the morning. The *food is love* hour.

But.

But back then they were looking out the train window at the sweet little French family squabbling over suitcases on the platform with the strings of coloured bulbs behind them. Somewhere like Spotorno along the Riviera di Ponente. Why wouldn't you want to be there? Where his family came from. Somewhere around this coast.

He was talking too fast. The little family reminded him of his aunt's family that spent the summer holidays at his grandmother's house on the seaside somewhere in New Zealand.

'. . . always forming a little ruck so they could squabble over something . . .'

Ruck?

And then in mid sentence he just blurted, 'Fuck it!'

She immediately knew why. He yanked the blind down as the train began to move, the compartment door's blind as well, and when he turned around from doing that she already had her knickers off and her frock hoisted, his mouth fell open like a big kid's and he let out a peculiar sound halfway between a cheer and a cry of pain, a kind of yodel. Probably she'd done something not dissimilar herself. Comical.

But nothing to do with his confidence act. No bravado. You didn't forget such *naked* moments – not in the sense of stripping off, it was more about dropping your guard than your knickers.

The long, rattling night, the bottles of *Rossese di Dolceacqua*, the station at Genoa, the guard banging on the compartment door.

'We have to come back to Genoa, Pepper, we have to eat

a *Cappon Magro*. That's just the kind of thing we have to do. That's a my-people kind of thing. A my-kind-of-thing people. Us Ligurian Maoris, Pepper. Bloody old Bob can go to hell. Fuck him. It's my shout.'

His red, wet, grinning mouth.

'What's a *Cappon Magro*? What do you mean, *shout*?'

'My treat.' He was opening another of Bob's sample bottles. 'No, you're my treat. Hot pepper.'

His rather large prick, trying valiantly.

'Enough, Christopher. Give it a rest, poor thing.'

'*Chris-to-pher*.' He was mocking the way she said his name, la-de-dah.

Grubby, purplish dawn over the industrialised Italian farmland on the last stretch towards Venice. The gash in his elbow from throwing the wine bottle out the window into the fields.

Of course all the signs were there. His up-and-downness and everything. The trick of his confidence and what happened to him when he couldn't find it.

But at the moments when she considered the pale little wretch in a hotel mirror, with the rather *triste* smile that only she was ever allowed to see, or admitted to herself that her feeling of slightly revolted apprehension at his cloddishness was the only grown-up reaction she should really be having to this affair – still, at these moments, she rebelled at her own boring common sense. She wanted that moment of utter nakedness again. His relish and naïve gusto, his delight, his life.

His *undeniableness*. His *right now*-ness.

Parker: *I've been running around in circles*.

Had she ever encountered anything like this *sensation*? He made her laugh, then he irritated her, he was infuriating and a bore, then he was brilliant, and finally when she whipped her knickers off while his back was turned in the train somewhere between Ventimiglia and Genoa it was because he made her want to do it.

Simple as that, he did it to her. That wasn't hard to admit, nothing to be ashamed of.

But before long there was the other aspect. A bit later, after the horrible row in Venice, his shitty behavior at the little *risotto nero* restaurant. And then his mouth like a squashed crimson fig, blubbering. *What am I supposed to do with this . . . feeling!*

Because at that moment it was also about her. She was beginning to be inside his *undeniable* perimeter, his faux confidence. The balance shifted. She was doing and she was also responding. Something like that.

Taking photographs in the Rialto markets, the bright-eyed sardines and the rattling, salty cascade of mussels, Christopher's anxious, swivelling head looking about for her in the crowd. At that moment she felt herself pause, and the nature of her *participation* shifted into another phase.

She could go back there and replay the sequences as though they were song lyrics or the proof sheets of photographs. Pick her way through them. *There*. Or maybe there. That one.

Play it again. *I've been running around in circles.*

It wasn't any longer a question of Christopher hastily pulling down the railway compartment blinds and his trousers, revealing his big eager cock. It was also her admitting that he'd woken her up again to her own ability to *act*. To do anything. To *look*.

Clumsy, ridiculous, funny, undeniable Christopher, hairy and out of proportion. And herself, after Venice, Thé Glacé. Ridiculous, what a pair they then became.

Beauty and the Beast, said Bob.

But when was that moment? When he wasn't any longer just *having an effect* on her? Waking her up? When did *the two of us* happen? When was it? When did that happen?

Somewhere along the schedule between *food is love* at Le Baratin in Paris and the little fish place in Venice. Between the *joues de boeuf* and the *risotto nero*.

Or was it between his pouty lips saying '*joues de boeuf*' in Bob's office in South Kensington and then spluttering '. . . this *feeling*!' in the hotel in Venice?

Or between her noticing her neighbour playing skank music and being an elephant to get his little girl to eat, in Wandsworth, and the horrid chill that made her seize up with fury when Christopher suggested she could be his column's Thé Glacé, in Venice?

Or between flushing away the remains of raspberry-coloured coke that would wreck her last chance, and finishing off the glass of turpentiney *pinot grigio* he'd sneered at?

Around and around, the chorus that wouldn't stop repeating. *Yeah you left me in another grey area*.

After that, after whenever *that* happened, the two of them together, there was always a kind of tussle going on. Sometimes moody, sometimes fun. When it worked it was *brilliant, brilliant*.

But when it didn't work she just felt this ghastly claustrophobia. As if she could only ever amount to anything when they were doing their famous double act. Beauty and the Beast, Pepper and Hare, *Thé Glacé and Rosenstein*, for the love of God.

And then there was another question and an answer she knew and sometimes saw in that wistful mirror.

Had she ever encountered anything *undeniable* like this before?

Of course she had.

There was poor little Dan, curled like a parenthesis around the beginning of a time in her life that had seemed like an awful endless waiting to be closed off, finished with, *got over*, an endlessly deferred or failed or missed return to sensation. The billboards along the overland railway line out to Goldsmiths at New Cross: 'Got Commitment Issues?' 'Time to Move On?'

Yes, so pathetic really, how could she admit it even to

herself when it felt almost shameful? But it was true, it was that big squalid parenthesis of Christopher curled against her back making little flubbery noises while he slept. Yes it was Christopher still asleep late in the morning after the huge ridiculous *Cappon Magro* in Boccadasse.

Not *food is love,* but close.

Mangiare è *fare l'amore!*

It was Christopher who'd closed down the undeniable time of poor little Danny, and the long undeniable denial that came after him. Yes it was thanks to Christopher that she could bear to remember Danny again, after ten years learning not to think about him.

Just started art school and she had her first taste, the lovely Israeli boy Dan very carefully tied off her pathetic little white arm and slipped the needle into her blue vein.

'Just like lapis lazuli, Mary, you should see it one day, blue like in the Chagall windows at the Hadassah in Jerusalem.'

How was she supposed to tell him she had? Been there, seen that? And Danny's thin, tender face, leaning over her.

'Okay Mary? It's good?'

Yes, it was, it was good, it was really, really good, and Danny was sweet, he looked after her very gently. When she was stoned, she was in a cocoon, a kind of time capsule, lovely.

But then the day protest posters went up at Goldsmiths. About the massacre of Palestinians in the Shatila and Sabra refugee camps in Beirut, it was September 1982. The posters were all along the corridor by the canteen and the courtyard. They had a photograph of a pile of bodies in a narrow alleyway, with a blood-red text saying *The truth: 2,000 dead civilians,* and the next time she saw Danny his sweet tenderness had gone. He was walking up and down, up and down in his posh flat, he was all sinews and tears, crying and ranting.

Saying over and over, 'How can they say it was the Jews,

it wasn't us, it was those Lebanese Christians, it was those fucking Arabs doing it to each other!'

But she could see he also knew what people were saying. That it was true, that he knew. His pain showed clearly that he knew the truth.

At that moment, trying to hold his jangling, angry body still for a moment, she'd felt her *sensation* of Danny shift. It wasn't any more just about him and his tenderness towards her with the heroin, and her need. It was also about her participation.

It was about the fact that he knew what she knew. That was when she was able to go inside his undeniableness to where he wasn't in control at all.

Graham Parker, Joe Jackson, Elvis Costello, Joy Division – Ian Curtis, 'Love will tear us apart'. As well as smack he turned her on to all that music.

His favourite Joe Jackson songs. *They say two hearts should beat as one for us.*

But she hadn't known enough to see what he would do, finally. The little knobbly body discarded, the overdose clichés arranged like a dreadful didactic display. Not a lot of vomit, just enough to make the point, and the apparatus all there rather tidily.

The thing she remembered vividly afterwards was that he only had one shoe on as if he'd been in too much of a hurry to get really comfortable. Poor rich little Dan. He'd always liked nice shoes and the one he'd taken off, one of his dressy chisel-toed Rogani Bruno e Francos was there, lined up all by itself on the floor outside his wardrobe, pathetic.

At Goldsmiths, someone kept tearing the posters down while others put fresh ones up with even more horrible images. Then someone defaced the posters with swastikas and wrote *PLO Nazis*. Arguments broke out around the Red Crescent Relief Fund table in the corridor with the black and white tiles, someone was always tipping it over. There were students wearing *keffiyeh* scarves around their necks in solidarity with the victims of the camps.

One day after Danny's funeral all the tiles in the black-and-white corridor shifted into three dimensions, the black ones on the bottom and the white ones floating just above them. She fell over and couldn't stand up again. The people who helped her out into the courtyard didn't understand what she was telling them about the leafy tree there, how its swirly branches made her feel sick.

She got out of the building and down Clifton Rise to the park, where she lay face down in the wet grass. Some Nigerians from the taxi co-op on the Rise found her there when they came down for a joint just after dark. They carried her up to the Montego Bay Spice Restaurant that Danny used to love. Its smell of fatty chicken made her retch. The owner sat her outside on a chair. Then the ambulance took her to A&E at Greenwich.

When her mother visited the Serenity clinic in Camden she brought letters with reports rebutting the Shatila and Sabra massacres from her sister, Auntie Ruth, in Jerusalem, but what did she care? What difference did it make?

Her father never visited, not that time or subsequently.

'Dan shall be a serpent by the road, a viper by the path, that bites the horses' heels.' This was the little prayer she said for Danny in the weeks afterwards, over and over, her first time in rehab. The text was in a brochure from her trip to Israel, the Dan Window at the Hadassah had a serpent coiling up a candlestick, she remembered it.

But she'd never told Danny that her parents had paid for her to go to Israel in the year before art school, to be with her mother's sister and her cousins.

And why was that, why hadn't she told Danny? Because it would have reminded him that he wasn't *there,* where he belonged, in Israel. In spite of everything he said about the place, the little rich boy, with his nice flat, his shoes, his drugs, he was just another rich brat, Danny, he was *just like her.* Except he looked Jewish and she didn't, peaches and cream, whatever that was supposed to mean. Poor Danny-the-viper's skinny little English *shiksa,* so he thought, with the lapis lazuli veins.

But she *was* Jewish, at least her family was, how else did you know? When she was young her parents had famous parties, Bianca Jagger came to one. She sat on the stairs and smoked pot with another woman who kept shouting 'No, no, no, you don't get it, Janka!'

Another time she saw David Hockney necking with a man in the kitchen while pouring a drink with his free hand. His owlish eyes behind his glasses were completely focused on the drink, not the man he was kissing.

They didn't observe Sabbath and didn't go to synagogue but they did have a family party at Yom Ha'atzmaut to celebrate the independence of Israel. They'd phone her mother's sister in Jerusalem, and her father would start a new fund-raising year with wine glasses raised around the table in a toast to the Jewish homeland.

But she just never bothered to tell Danny. Or she did, once, at a gig in Venue on New Cross Road by the college, only it was too loud for him to hear what she was saying and she knew it. Anyway he was singing along with Joe Jackson and he was stoned out of his mind. *Don't you feel like breaking out or breaking us in two?*

And then all those years, finishing at art school, the magazine work, trapped between two images: poor little Danny with one shoe off and his head tipped sideways into the vomit on his shoulder, and the piled-up corpses at the end of the alleyway in the Beirut refugee camp.

One image so neat and deliberate, despite the shoe, the other one a panicky mess.

Sometimes she got out, there were really good times, the money was phenomenal during the '90s, they were all having lots of fun. And then without warning she'd be back in the space between Danny and the dead Palestinians.

No *sensation*, that awful, magic word.

But that usually saw her back at Serenity, shovelling her trust funds into their bank account.

And then, one day, there was Christopher looking at her with his mooncalf eyes, his delirious smile, over the absurd pile of food on the platter between them, near Genoa.

That other *food is love* moment – the other *big question* moment.

The *Cappon Magro* was the silliest thing she'd seen in her entire life, but how could she tell Christopher that? Boccadasse was quaint, the colourful houses, the narrow streets, the fishing boats, lots of seafood restaurants. The Santa Chiara was a particularly lovely one, and Christopher so wanted her to love it. The owners were Christopher's friends, maybe even relatives. The man, Luigi, pinched Christopher's cheek and called him *cuginetto*, while the woman, Luisa, performed an eloquent little head-rock and went back to her kitchen.

'Yes, we prepare special for you, after my little cousin telephone, Luisa work all day, a special *Cappon* for the bride of my savage cousin from New Zealand.'

She'd caught Christopher's quick look, then, almost apprehensive. He was waiting for a reaction, but she let it pass – *bride* – thinking it was just the owner's English.

Christopher was still being sorry after the *risotto nero* incident and his 'big question' faux pas back in Venice. They were meant to go on to London after Venice but he insisted they *had to* come all the way back to Genoa so he could make it up to her for the Thé Glacé fiasco. Bob would be furious – the delays, the cost, but most of all the *gall*.

After all the lovely grubby wine and sex on the sleeper going north the return trip was utterly miserable. The train was completely overbooked in the best Italian manner. By the time they got to Genoa they were exhausted. And then, outside yet another of Christopher's 'amazingly cheap' hotels, there were noisy machines doing road improvements first thing in the morning.

'Don't be so grumpy, Pepper.' He was frowning at her over his cup of coffee, but trying not to. His coat collar was turned up. It was blowy and gritty in the square and some Arab truck drivers were smoking smelly cigarettes at the table next to them. She thought the pigeons looked diseased, squabbling over the pastry she hadn't liked.

'Bob's going to have a fit.'

'But here you are.'

Yes, she was. And she'd hardly been kidnapped. She'd said yes. They did this all day. Back and forth, not quite quarrelling. He was trying not to be grumpy with her. Really, she wished she was going home to London, and he wished she would love whatever he was up to. But she couldn't work out what that was. What he was being so secretive about.

'Oh, come on, Christopher – what are you cooking up?'

'It's a secret, Pepper.' That hopeful smile. 'You'll see.' He pressed both her hands, made pouty kisses. 'You'll love it.'

Love what?

They ate some tasteless octopus terrine standing up at a booth near the ugly industrial port. He had that slightly beseechy look. She didn't even like it let alone love it, the octopus terrine. Her feet were killing her. But the octopus lunch wasn't the big secret surprise, obviously. Just as well.

Then they looked at some paintings by Caravaggio in the Palazzo Rosso because he thought they would 'cheer her up'. She could have made fun of the suggestion that Caravaggio might cheer anyone up, but that would have sounded know-all and snotty.

There was an immense, devouring field of darkness at the back of Caravaggio's *Ecce Homo* and she panicked when she saw that the young model for Christ looked like Danny. The tender, downcast eyes, wispy beard, young hairless body. The last thing she needed in her life at that point: a tragic Danny cue.

And then in the evening, after a nasty windy walk along the Corso to Boccadasse, this enormous plate on the table in front of her. Glasses being filled with wine, Christopher's eyes brimming over with joy and happiness, and the sudden sound of clapping from Luigi and Luisa when Christopher lifted his glass to her and tried to control his shaking lips.

'What is it, Christopher?'

'It's a Cap-, Cap-, *Cappon Magro*, Pepper.'

She'd never heard him stammer before. His eyes flooded and the tears poured out down his cheeks and into his trembling grin.

'No, Christopher, don't be silly, I know what *that* is. You've told me. Don't be such a dolt. I mean, what's . . . ?'

'Sorry,' he gasped, swabbing his eyes with his napkin. 'I'm just . . .' Then he swallowed about half his glass of wine at a gulp. 'Thé Glacé . . . will you marry me? Miss Pepper? Please?'

In front of her there'd been an enormous pile of green beans, cauliflower, potatoes, carrots, celery hearts, artichokes, beetroots, hard-boiled eggs, white fish, dark dried tuna, lobster and scampi, mussels, cockles, oysters on half shells, anchovies, black and green olives, mushrooms, all on a bed of thick toast. There were half a dozen skewers poking up out of the pyramid with more bug-eyed scampi, mushrooms and anchovies impaled on them. The whole catastrophe was bathed in glistening sauce.

'Will you, Pepper?'

His friends had appeared on either side of him, with full glasses. The aroma that was rising from the absurd *Cappon Magro* was indescribably delicious. But she couldn't tell if that was what made her feel faint, or if it was something like the awful darkness at the back of Caravaggio's *Ecce Homo* with its sad, lovely portrait of the wilted, almost beardless boy with his head drooping to one side.

But then, at the very moment she couldn't hold her huge sob back any longer, just as she was going to pass out or disappear into the deep darkness behind Danny, she saw Christopher's big moppy head loom into view above the pile of food. He looked so comically a part of it that her sob turned back on itself and became a sort of whoop.

'Food is love!' – the arrogance of the man.

The *Cappon Magro*: there it had sat between them with its absurd palisade of skewers stuck with prawns and mushrooms. It had always been between them. But how could she have told him that then? When his 'food is love' story about his wretched Italian grandmother was so desperately trying to join them together? How could she have known what was going to happen?

Desperate, desperate, desperate Christopher. Desperate for love. Love that admired him. Love that made all of him swell up, not just his big bulgy cock. Love that would always come to his rescue.

Christopher's cry for help: 'Food is love!'

Well, not her, not this time, not any more. Let alone when the cry came via some Maya Yazbeck – 'A message from your husband.' Let *her* prop the poor clod up. Whoever she was.

Back then in Boccadasse, they'd been laughing and crying all over each other and all over Luigi and Luisa and half the guests in the restaurant.

But had she said yes?

Her strange whoop.

Yes, of course she'd said yes.

They drank toasts to food and love. *Mangiare è fare l'amore!*

And of course the ribald jokes – *Cos'e che ti rode!*

Before they devoured the *Cappon Magro* she photographed

it. Once by itself, looking like an outrageous, mocking art work, a revoltingly excessive still life of some sort. And once with Luigi, Luisa and Christopher raising their glasses to her, with the *Cappon* crouched in front of them. Its hackles up.

Of course she could never be in the photographs she took, except as a kind of absent reflection, the ghost of decision – or indecision. Of course she'd said yes. Yes to Christopher, yes to taking the photograph. It was her *yes* that they were raising their glasses to, that they were all beaming at, Christopher most of all, just beside himself, exuberant and ecstatic.

But she wasn't in the picture. She wasn't there, that's what struck her when she looked at the test-strip, back in London. Not there – Thé Glacé, Mary Pepper, not there. Didn't anyone, not least her, think it was worthwhile putting her in the picture? Luigi or Luisa could have photographed her and Christopher, with the *Cappon*. It was as though the *Cappon Magro* had taken her place and also the place of her *yes*.

When the jackhammers started up outside their hotel window the next morning after the *Cappon* feast at Boccadasse, Christopher didn't move. He lay against her back, his lips vibrating gently. His breath puffed moistly onto her shoulder blade. There was a sweet, delicate taste in her mouth, not fishy and not like the artichokes or cauliflower, and not rich like shellfish. She'd eaten a whole lot of the *Cappon*, heaps – it was indescribably delicious – and Christopher was thrilled about that.

But she'd never been able to tell him how bizarre, how ghastly it had looked when Luigi, with a grand flourish, had first put it on the table between them.

Never.

How it had reared up hideously over her sob, her whoop, her *yes*, with its skewers of black-eyed scampi and the pallid sheen on its flanks. How it seemed to have stationed itself at the centre of her fucked-up life.

She had this comical flashback of Christopher chiding

Peter Gordon at the Sugar Club in London: 'It doesn't look like food any more, treasure. It looks like fucking art. Sensational art, but art.'

The poor *Cappon* had looked like the worst kind of parody of what Peter Gordon was doing, those artful fusion arrangements that Christopher was mocking as 'fucking art'.

Sensational art.

Perhaps she'd gone back to sleep, then, she wasn't sure. She slid somewhere between sensation and dreaming. It was nearly midday when Christopher woke up. Outside, the road repair machines had stopped. At first it seemed to be completely silent. Then she could hear people, pigeons, scooters.

She felt Christopher give a startled twitch and lift his scratchy cheek from her back. Then he relaxed, and she could just picture the absurd, blissful smile on his face.

And.

And she still could.

CHAPTER 6

Hawwa Habash stepped back quickly from the door she had locked against the image of the food writer Christopher Hare's imploring expression. His face was large as you would expect from someone whose work was to eat, but she thought the largeness did not come from eating but from an excess of personality, so that there was much room for confusion. At one moment this excess was of boldness and humour, at the next it was of sadness and indecision. At first she had thought his problem was bravado and stupidity, but now she had seen the grief and hope in his expression, his big-lipped mouth hanging open towards her as she shut the door, his hands open to make the sign of a question. And what was that question?

Clearly it related to what he had said, in that calm way, with honesty that pierced her, though she knew better than to show it: *this is the present. This is the only place from which I can go forward.*

Yes, she understood that. She understood it in the arid depths of her soul, that well into which no *shaduf* had been able to reach for years, from which no refreshment could be lifted out into the day.

And also that he had attached his hope to her – this hopeless man.

It startled her that when she turned from locking the door Philippe was standing on the stairs two or three steps below the landing. The image of the food writer's imploring expression had not yet dissipated, and it seemed to float across the implacable face of Philippe, a face she knew it was wise to fear. He stood with both arms extended to the side, one hand holding the banister and the other's fingers spread against the wall. How long had he been there? At least he had not been listening at the door. His location was surely deliberate: she knew Philippe well enough to understand his succinct drama, his message to her.

But still she gasped when she saw him there. He lifted his shoulders and eyebrows in a question, ignoring her fright. His manner was even somewhat brutal.

This is the only place from which I can go forward. She stopped Philippe's commanding question with one hand while opening the door to the room she had slept in the night before. She closed the door on Philippe's anger just as, moments before, she had closed another on the food writer's open mouth, his *how?* or *quoi?*, his sad hands empty of answers. *How can I go forward?*

In the room she rushed to take a pillow from the bed and catch her groans in it.

Was it any longer an issue of her authenticity? No, she had not been brought up in the squalor of Shatila but in a comfortable house in Amman. Her family had not walked in the terrible heat to Barfiliya at the time of *al-Nakba* and the invasion of Lydda in 1948, but had left a week earlier and escaped to Amman, taking the deed box and the key to the house, and taking also her grandmother's future performances and commemorations during the bad-tempered conclusion of the *hamseen.* And no, as she herself had never denied, as Philippe knew well, she had not been in Shatila in 1982 when the Kataeb entered the camp under the patronage of the Israelis and defiled many young women and mothers her age, rather she had been for whole days and nights happily in the fresh marriage bed of her new husband

Abdul Yassou, in the small apartment on rue Lepic provided by her brother Habib, to keep his disgraceful sister under the eyes of her family who might have been better advised to disown her, as he was fond of repeating. Since her marriage had been a hasty affair, conducted hastily for all the world to see in the official French manner in the *mairie* on the rue du Faubourg Saint-Martin, which was, it hardly needed to be said, a long way from Amman, without her father or mother present, and without Abdul Yassou's father also, and without any suggestion of a subsequent ceremony in the church on Jebel Ashrafieh in Amman and without a week of celebrations hosted by her father, and without a dowry – as a consequence of this display of indifference the only siege she had suffered was that of her own brother's vigilance.

And what of her own defilement, for which her brother had been obliged to take responsibility on account of his earlier inattention, though his attention to one careless impromptu had been sufficient to expose her affair with Abdul Yassou? *That* she had agreed to, the affair, willingly and rebelliously, and in due course with pleasure, after many months of secret courtship by handsome Abdul Yassou. It had been her choice, to defy the codes of her family and embrace those of her friends at the Jussieu campus.

Abdul Yassou loathed the apartment for its degrading size, its enslavement of his honour and its proximity to the filthy Africans of the Goutte d'Or, as he would often complain – and as he did also about the dowry. But that did not prevent him from relishing his newly legitimate bride, and it did not prevent her from rejoicing in her rebellion and in his connoisseurship in their bed.

And it was the case, on the day of the massacres of Sabra and Shatila in Beirut, that the lovemaking cries of Hawwa and Abdul Yassou in Paris caused their neighbours to complain or perhaps to celebrate by banging cooking pots together in the hallway of the apartment building and on the balcony next door, where the windows were open day and night because of the fierce summer heat. And, indeed, perhaps it was the case that during those roasting days and nights of unrestrained passion, of clashing pans and complaints, of Abdul Yassou's big hands gently lifting her loins towards his patience, that their son Boutros was conceived. Indeed it was possible he was conceived on the very day of the Shatila and Sabra massacres and defilements, a stupid thought whose melodrama she despised, which did not prevent it returning often to twist her heart.

But she could not deny it: it was then that the vivid years of her life began, when she inhabited every day to its very limits, when Boutros had at last slithered out of her in a rush of blissful fluids, when she had sung in the mornings, when her hot arguments with Abdul Yassou had ended in love-making, when she was always alive, minute by minute. A *presentness* that she had subsequently dragged around, wishing to be free of it, and now perhaps at last she might be.

Of course there were signs even then, in the time of her rebellious happiness. She was young but she was not stupid. She saw her husband's rage at the lost dowry, which suggested he had wanted it. And, in spite of the withheld dowry, the ample money he often had. His residency permit for San Marino, where he did not live, but banked, so it seemed. His anger when the PLO forces of Yasser Arafat evacuated Lebanon in August 1982, the first month of her womanly bliss – was this because the *fedayeen* were now admitting defeat and betraying the Palestinian cause, because they were abandoning those left helpless and without defense in the ruins of the refugee camps? No, for Abdul Yassou it was because of the billions of capital owned by the PLO that would now flee the country, and the cessation of remittances to PLO banks in Beirut. The cessation of arms shipments to Sidon and Tyre. The retiring of Lebanese-French banks from that place. The inflation that had already begun as a consequence.

Abdul Yassou did not mention the *difficulty* of doing business with the Phalange of Gemayel, the same who had perpetrated the massacres of Palestinians at Shatila and Sabra. This business she only discovered many years later, when Philippe placed the dossier of her husband on a table in front of her and invited her to read it in front of him, Philippe, while he watched.

Had she known? What had she known? Philippe saw from her behaviour that she had not known, and that was also perhaps why he agreed that she should be the one to shoot Abdul Yassou. Why perhaps he had already seeded the possibility that she might propose this herself, the justified execution of her husband Abdul Yassou. Her handsome lover Abdul Yassou who had smiled so insolently when her brother Habib by chance opened the door when he should have been at work, and saw them. Abdul Yassou the father of her beautiful son, Boutros, rest his soul, her baby who might already have begun to exist that day or others not long before.

She had not wanted to argue with Abdul Yassou at this time, the time of their romance and marriage, but he saw her doubts and took care to soothe them. Was he not a businessman after all, he murmured, one who had to live by his own wits, since her family had decided to mistrust him? And was he not a businessman in Lebanon, where business was conducted in the old ways? And what, he whispered, caressing her, were they now to stage their own civil war, like the one that had ruined Beirut and his own father?

Yes, she had known something, but not everything. Yes, he had come and gone without much explanation from Amman after her graduation and return there in 1983. He said it was because her family still did not welcome him without reservation in their house. Yes, his legitimate rage was on behalf of Boutros when she left the child with her maid and went to Beirut that year and was present when the

US Embassy was bombed. *What was she thinking?* She did not even know the answer herself. And, yes, he had reasons for taking Boutros away to Paris when she again left him with the maid and went to Beirut in 1986. And who could blame him for being armed when her brothers came to Paris to recover the child he loved just as passionately as she did?

And even then, in those difficult times, she was still living in that presentness.

But was she so crazy then to want to take her work where it was needed? Was he to be punished for loving his own son and fearing the zeal of his crazy wife? These were not unreasonable questions, even to this day. And the years after she agreed to return to Paris with him in the spring of 1988, to complete her specialist *pédiatrique* at l'Hôpital Robert Debré, their enjoyment of excursions with Boutros in Buttes Chaumont and la Villette, the apartment they were comfortable in with her deferred dowry – were these the years not of her happiness but of her delusion? Were their special nights out at Le Baratin on rue Jouye-Rouve close to their apartment also a delusion? Was she incapable of seeing what her husband did?

No, she was not. She was not incapable of seeing it. But there were limits to what she knew about him and what he did, and these were not limits she chose to impose on her knowledge. They existed, she saw them, she did not deny them, but she left them alone. And this was because she saw that there were no limits, no there were none, to what she knew about his love for Boutros. She spent her days at Robert Debré in the *urgences pédiatriques* looking into the faces of anxious love, she knew their expression. So perhaps she also chose to accept that whatever she did not know about her husband was overruled by that expression she saw on his face when his lips reached down to the cheek of their sleeping Boutros, by the terror she saw there on the face of a father, the hope that this child might always be safe.

Every month they would get somewhat drunk at Le Baratin because it was congenial and Abdul Yassou liked the heavy Argentinian wine and the rich meat dishes, and afterwards they would dismiss the babysitter and make love – was she not justified to hope, on this evidence, that their happiness was permitted? And also, if she did not inquire too closely about the nature of his business trips, was that not least because of the rigours of her medical studies and her duties as a young mother?

It was twenty-one years after she had first shivered in anticipation at the sight of Abdul Yassou's fine teeth biting the thick Argentinian beefsteak at Le Baratin that Philippe put the dossier of Abdul Yassou on the table in front of her in the house in Amman. It was true, she did not deny it then or now, that time in her life with Abdul Yassou and Le Baratin had been a burden for many years, she had not escaped it. Philippe put the dossier on the table in Amman in the house that had been her father's, where she now lived when she was there, on Jebel Ashrafieh near the Orthodox church. She opened the dossier on the same old table where her grandmother had yearly required her father to place the deed box for the house in Lydda, the same table at which they had then eaten the yearly 'catastrophe' lunches. It was the same table across which the young Abdul Yassou had carefully regarded her from beneath his beautiful eyelashes, thirty-four years ago, when she was just a schoolgirl of sixteen and he a man of twenty-six.

And now nineteen years since Abdul Yassou had descended into something resembling a well poisoned with corpses when the only real love of his life died. When Boutros, their beautiful son, whose warm cheek his lips had touched with a father's fearful love, died.

This was her obsessive litany, the enumeration of her fate, the dates she counted again and again as if with a rosary.

But now, perhaps, *this is the only place from which I can*

go forward. Yes, but Abdul Yassou could not – not now, certainly, but neither from the moment nineteen years ago when his beloved Boutros died.

And could she, now? *Go forward?* But where?

She even smiled at the wet bite-mark and the dark lipstick on the pillow with which she had smothered her groans. In another circumstance it might be mistaken for a lover's signature. Indeed, perhaps it was, in a sense. As the poet Mahmoud Darwish wrote, 'Place my pillow on the wound.'

She even remembered the poet's face when he read those lines in the hall near Place de la République, his large tinted spectacles and mournful mouth, and the voice that was more sad than angry. The audience leaned forward in their seats and there was a murmuring throughout, as if many of those present were also repeating the words they heard inside themselves, connecting the words to where rough thyme grew in Galilee, at Birwa, near Acre, the poet's birthplace. Some of those in the audience would have trodden on that thyme, and forty years later smelled the words the poet recited in Paris – and others, like herself, smelled the place only in the poet's words, or in the words of her grandmother when she recited her account of the small garden in Lydda.

And when she spoke to the poet about this, he said that yes, there were two exiles, one from the place and another from the memory of it, and his poems were always losing their way between the two; that was their meaning.

She did her best to clean her face and refresh her body using bottled mineral water and a towel, not wishing to reveal her condition on the way to the bathroom where the food writer had performed so ostentatiously. Perhaps Philippe had by now returned to the room downstairs to wait for her, or perhaps he was still waiting out there on the landing. She did not want him to see on her face the stain of her grief, as she had often seen it on the faces of mothers and fathers, when she was a young doctor who would sometimes go and sit alone in Nôtre Dame de Fatima near the *urgences pédiatriques*, to compose herself.

She brushed her teeth with the mineral water, and spat into a cup, then applied fresh makeup and some perfume. That would have to do, though soon she would stand under a hot shower in the service apartment in Geneva, for as long as she wanted, and put on fresh clothes. And cease to conceal herself within the identity of the singer Maya Yazbeck, for the love of God.

Now Philippe had to listen to her. She would make him, because this was the moment at which events would inevitably move forward, this was *the only place from which I can go forward*, and he had agreed that she had the right to propose a direction, to make her choice before the arrival of Antun in the morning, which was now already not so far away.

When she came into the room downstairs, Philippe was there sitting at the table and smoking a cigarette. He extinguished it when he heard her come in, as was his polite manner, but he did not look at her until she had sat down opposite him. And even then, he did not alter his disposition or move his head but merely caught her eyes with his, as if he had been gazing all along at the exact space where her face would appear. There was no expression on his face and, having stubbed out the cigarette, he folded that hand over the other and looked at her as if she had been there all along. She had brought in a bottle of arrack and another of water, with two rinsed glasses, but Philippe did not change his expression when she poured two drinks and put one in front of him. He inclined his head just a little in thanks, but did not lift the glass to his lips.

Outside, the *sanitaire* went past slowly and she waited until the sound of the truck's engine and its rushing water had passed – yes, the night was almost over. How often as a young mother and a weary young student doctor in Paris she had risen at the sound of the *sanitaire* to study for an hour or two before Boutros woke and needed his breakfast.

Then the truck turned the corner of the street and the silence in the room seemed to emanate from Philippe, from his patience, but also perhaps his menace. She took a swallow of the cloudy aniseed and began to sing directly into Philippe's silence, the well-known song of Oum Kalthoum, 'Alf Layla Wa Layla', some short verses from it which he surely knew. Everybody knew that song.

You took me in love in the blink of an eye
and you showed me where the sweetest days are
the sweetest days, the sweetest days
and the desert of my life became a garden

My love, let us live in the night's eyes
and tell the sun come over, come after one year not before,
come over, come over, come over, come over,
after one year but not before

In a sweet night of love
in one thousand and one nights
one thousand and one
one thousand and one nights
in one thousand and one nights
one thousand and one
one thousand and one nights

They say it is life
what is life but a night like tonight
like tonight, tonight, like tonight

The tears that ran down her cheeks caught in the corners of her mouth, and she did not restrain them. As she sang the last lines, her mouth was salted and moistened by the tears which also dripped from her chin on to the table in front of her. Water was running from her nose, and she let it. It was that heavy, burdensome *present* of so many years that now seemed to leave her, to rush out of her, as Boutros had left her body, and then the afterbirth, all at once a freedom from effort she could never have imagined.

Then Philippe lifted his glass of arrack and took a sip, but still his expression remained a kind of silence. In front of him, Hawwa Habash wept without restraint as she had never imagined she could except at the death of her little *habibi*, her beloved Boutros, the beloved also of Abdul Yassou.

She waited, inside the silent gaze of Philippe, until she could speak again.

'I have been the fate of Abdul Yassou who was my husband, and before that I was the destiny of our child, as God knows, and now you are asking me to take the fate of this food writer upstairs in my hands also?'

Philippe did not answer her, so she continued. 'I will tell you what this man said to me, this fool as we all believe him to be, this *problem*. To me, when he saw what fate might propose for him, when I had explained it, he said, *this is the present. This is the only place from which I can go forward*. This was not a complicated thought, but for him a profound one. What I saw in him was what I have seen many times in the faces of those looking at their own decisions to live or die, or how to live or die, or when.'

She thought Philippe was about to interrupt her at this moment so she raised her finger to her lips to stop him – but he simply took another sip of his arrack and waited.

'There is a certain moment when the doctor must depart and leave the decision with the person who owns it. There is for all of us fortunate to have become adults a place of balance where our life tips this way or that. For Abdul Yassou, the *shaduf* tipped the day our son Boutros was killed.'

Now Philippe lifted his hand as if to say 'Stop', but she reached across and pressed his hand back on the table.

'Now, Philippe, you have to let me speak until I have finished.'

He placed his other hand on top of the one with which she had restrained his interruption. She felt its warmth, but there was little enough warmth in his face.

'Yes, that day he blamed me, and not without reason; he beat me and broke my arm, he held his gun to my head, his face was black. That was his *present*, Philippe, you must know this, there was no other, this present was always with him after that, so how could he go forward? Yes, he was already for a long time a crook and a collector of bribes and *rashwa*, no better or worse perhaps than all those who profited from that war in Lebanon, from the great *zaim* down to those *mokhtar* who issued passports from their barber shops. But what he became after that day was worse, as you know, and the bad got worse. He could not stop it, and so it had to be stopped. That was not a decision he could make.'

Opposite her, Philippe made a rocking motion with one forearm braced against the other. 'Yes, sister,' he murmured, 'what will the *shaduf* lift from the well?'

Then he smiled, just a little, and made a joke. 'Not, at any rate, the voice of Oum Kalthoum, in your case. Nor, thank God, that of Maya Yazbeck.'

She thought he must be mocking her archaic figure of speech in the *shaduf*, and certainly he was mocking her singing, but how else could she speak of something at once so old and so familiar? The old lever that lifted water from a well was how she visualised that moment when fate and decision met across the fulcrum. And how many songs had been sung and were still composed every day in which the sun was begged to slow its passage so the night of love might go on, go on, go on – that the *present* might stop still? Her own decisions had tipped her fate, and then she had moved on only because she was blessed with work and the thanks for it that appeased her guilt and grief. But what had Abdul Yassou had? A heart that was poisoned, from which his rage could never drain away.

Now Philippe stood up wearily; he was after all a man of seventy who had sustained his command of their project for many weeks now, on insufficient sleep. This time it was his turn to stop her from speaking. He placed his finger on his lips, which were almost smiling, again as if gently mocking her. 'A moment,' he said. 'One moment, Oum Boutros.' Then she knew with certainty that he was not mocking, and her heart gave a sad thump in her chest – she could feel this long night approaching its conclusion.

When he came back it was with a towel, a napkin, and a bowl of warm water scented with eau de cologne. He made her turn her chair so he could carefully bathe her face. She could smell his cigarettes, and that he, too, had not changed his clothes since that morning. He gently cleaned her face as he might the hot, tear-stained face of a granddaughter. She closed her eyes while he did so, and then felt his kiss on her forehead, and the towel he folded across her hands. As she dried her face and hid her emotion a little longer inside the towel, she heard his chair scrape back on the other side of the table. And then his voice, quiet as usual, factual, without emotion, the voice of an engineer or perhaps a surgeon, calmly listing the necessities of the moment.

'To remind you, my friend, because you need to believe the truth, that what you have done is just. That man you were brave enough to shoot, risking your own life and your future, was no longer your husband – and I would say he was also no longer the father of your son. You may not agree with me, but listen. You say there is a moment when the thing tips, whatever it is, like a *shaduf* at the well. We call it fate when we do not wish to make the decision ourselves. But I would say that Abdul Yassou decided he was no longer the father of Boutros when he sold arms to both the Kataeb who are the enemies of Palestine, and to their enemies the *fedayeen*, his own people. And when he stole medical supplies from the Red Crescent at Barbir hospital in Beirut and then sold them back, when he imported spoiled food and sold it to the starving, when he accepted *rashwa* and kickbacks to launder the money of those *zaim* resident in Paris, and kept accounts in those other places where, as you know, he also kept women. And this was even in the year he married you, which was also the year your son was conceived. No, you did not know about these things, or not enough, but you know now that what he did after both the birth and the death of his son, whom of course he loved, was worse only in that it continued, not in degree.'

She removed the towel and saw then that, despite his calm voice, Philippe's face had become blotchy with rage, that his nose was white with it, and there was sweat glistening on his forehead.

'I would say, my poor friend, that the man you married was not the father of your child even before the child was conceived. And that this was his decision, despite his paternal gestures, his protestations, despite what you perceive to be his *fate*.'

He spat the last word, venomously, with rage, as though all the calmness in his voice had been preparing to detonate and now shot *fate* out, hissing like an artillery round. He reached across the table and took the towel from her.

'Excuse me,' he said, and mopped his face and neck. Then, as he never did in her company, he lit a cigarette, his hands shaking. 'And then, subsequently,' he said, 'as you know, the kidney harvests, those Syrian Jews in New Jersey, and even children, Palestinian ones . . .'

His careful factual voice had become disordered; he heard this and stopped. He waved the cigarette in apology and then stubbed it out. He took a large sip of his arrack. Calm blood began to return to his face.

This, too, had been a tipping moment.

She was not surprised by what he had said – she had even expected it, after the many days of his self-control, as their project came to its conclusion. Often she too had had to control her rage at the obscenity of the word 'harvest', as a doctor whose work was with poor children, and as the mother of a dead child. And now there was a different rapprochement in her relationship with Philippe, since he had finally showed her his emotion, which she had always known was what made him dangerous, not just his skill.

This she had to respect, and she did, with gratitude, although they would not see each other again once they had reached Italy in the morning and had gone their separate ways – she on the plane from Genoa to Geneva, to her appointment at the ILO, Mahfouz to sell the red saloon in Genoa, where it might once again become a taxi, even a white one.

And Philippe? Philippe she would see for the last time in her life, a dignified old man rolling a small wheeled suitcase into the railway station at Genoa, where the train went inland to Turin, where he would disappear. Then, before long, she would be taking her shower in the apartment in Geneva, with its closet of good clothes and some drawers of the plain things she liked, Doctor Hawwa Habash, to report on behalf of Regional Office Beirut. How was it now, in Gaza, for the children? And, Doctor, how was your holiday on the Côte d'Azur?

'Yes,' she said, 'but now in any case it does not matter, because he is dead, Abdul Yassou. But as for the food writer.'

'You must do what you have decided,' said Philippe. He was calm again, but tired – there was a little flicking in his left eyelid, and he lifted first by mistake the hand in which he held his glass, but next the free one, to rub the tic. 'Go, do it, I already support you. But I think we will leave earlier than we planned, before Antun arrives. I am not satisfied with that one.'

'I will talk to him one last time, this Christopher Hare.' Hawwa Habash lifted her glass to salute the tired old man on the other side of the table. '*Mabrouk*, Philippe, you are a good man. It has been my honour to work with you.'

'And you, Doctor.' He drained his glass and smiled. 'How long do you need?'

'One hour, no more.'

'Then I will sleep for one hour, no more.' As she expected, the hint of sarcasm. Philippe had recovered his guile. He put his glass upside-down on the table and lifted to his lips the little cross that hung on a chain around his neck. He bowed, the merest inclination, holding her eyes with his, correct and formal. Then he went to the stairs and ascended slowly, as if he had already begun to turn off the power to his body. She could see he was content with their decision.

But also, she could see what he had just done.

'And the one with whom you are not satisfied?'

Philippe paused in his careful ascent, but did not turn around. He answered, as if he were merely reminding himself of something she already knew, 'You mean the one left behind?'

Then he lifted his hand from the banister in a gesture of dismissal and went on to his rest.

Hawwa Habash sat alone in the unpleasant lower room of the building used by the Arab truck drivers and the importer of cheap Turkish kitchenware, furniture, and shoes, with its careless hygiene and the paper cover on the table greasy with chicken shashlik, and its pornographic calendar next to the shelves of canned goods, and its pot of scorched chickpeas and garlic that no-one had emptied and cleaned, and the pair of overalls greasy with diesel that had hung for two days on a hook behind the door to the garage at the back. She heard Philippe's door close firmly on the floor above, the one below the food writer. She knew that Philippe would sleep efficiently and wake with precision.

Yes, she understood what he had done, Philippe. He had left her with the *shaduf* of her decision and its consequences, that image he had gently mocked for its archaic sentimentality – he had even blessed the moment with his little gold cross and his courteous bow, his eyes holding hers because they were equals in responsibility.

But he had also accepted responsibility for her decision without asking to know its details or predicting its likely consequences. He was exposing his back to her decision and trusting her. This was the meaning of his wave. That he would walk from the railway station in Turin to wherever he was going, and not feel on his back the eyes of any police, nor those of the well-informed friends of Abdul Yassou, or those dealers in abominations in New Jersey, or the agents of the Kataeb in Beirut and Paris, or the Israeli *Shin Bet*, or the Syrian *Mukhabarat*, or the Lebanese *Deuxième Bureau*.

And mostly, that he would not be betrayed by any irresponsible 'fate' whose existence he had repudiated with such unique rage. There would be no 'fate'. There was only her decision which he had blessed so that he could now calmly sleep 'for one hour, no more'. And then leave her to continue with whatever had to be done next.

For example, in this instance, with *the one left behind*.

Before commencing a procedure at the Red Crescent hospital in Amman, or in the *cliniques pédiatriques* at Baqa'a, Balata, Deir el-Balah or the other camps, she would place her gloved hands on the sheet covering the child she was to operate on. She would breathe carefully and deeply, spread her fingers, and silently count on them the main points of her plan.

First: If Abdul Yassou was unguarded, the window seat of the restaurant was to have been left empty, as a signal that she could proceed; that was Antun's task. Second: had the food writer therefore been a decoy, to protect Abdul Yassou? Third: was Antun therefore in the employ of Abdul Yassou? Fourth: if so, he was a dead man, because he had failed. Because she had decided to do it anyway, to kill her husband, after checking the window from the other side of the road. Fifth: because now either the friends of Abdul Yassou would kill Antun for his failure to protect their comrade in crime, or, sixth, those of Philippe would do so for his betrayal of their cause. Seventh: but risks such as these were beyond the reach of Antun's weak character. So, eighth, it was likely that his action was either a foolish error, or, ninth, an attempt to prevent Abdul Yassou from becoming suspicious of the empty table.

This much was clear – she folded her hands on the table, but moved her tenth finger up and down, like a little *shaduf*: what, then, was the consequence of this?

If Antun had betrayed them to the police, they would have arrived at the truck drivers' house by now. But if he had done so, the police would also be content with the death of Abdul Yassou, in which case they would not hurry, and they would also be content with the death of Antun, who had signed his own death-warrant, because that would excuse them from further action, since their source of information would be stopped.

So, probably, he had not betrayed them to the police whose protection he knew better than to trust.

If he had already betrayed them to the friends of Abdul Yassou, on the other hand, then he was a dead man even sooner, because his usefulness was at an end while his untrustworthiness was now clear. This he would have known. So, probably, he had not betrayed them to the friends of Abdul Yassou – or not yet.

What would be Antun's chief fear? That he himself would be betrayed for his part in this procedure. That the safe circle of secrecy had been broken – by the food writer.

Therefore she would leave Antun to make his own decision. About what to do with the food writer. In any case, to accomplish the task of *the one left behind*.

She stopped the tapping of her finger, folding it in her other hand.

And the food writer, Christopher Hare, whose hands had resembled begging bowls empty of answers? Could she explain this to him? His excessive expression had been overflowing with the question *can you please show me the way?* This question was hidden inside his own words: *this is the only place from which I can go forward*. So he had already made his decision, he did it many hours ago when he ran after her, or ran after the present time he had lost – at any rate ran from the restaurant; and now only he could choose and discover where that decision would take him.

How could she tell him this?

CHAPTER 7

He woke from a kind of dream – unsure if he'd been sleeping – because of the noise. He couldn't believe it: they were singing downstairs! Or rather, the woman was. Going for it. These long phrases that twisted and turned. He'd heard that kind of stuff in restaurants all over the Middle East, and Edgeware Road for that matter, as well as from crackly loudspeakers above rickety tables on the jetty, where was it? With the grilled red snapper, and waves breaking against the riprap? And even at Ducasse's rubbishy Tamaris joint in Beirut, was there no stopping the guy? A woman's voice winding around and around, over an orchestra that sounded like a roomful of clowns rattling coat-hangers and blowing kazoos.

Only, to be fair, it was only her voice, this time: the doctor's, Hawwa Habash's, strong and not young, a bit hoarse, and though faint from where he was, obviously quite emotional. So not exactly a party, with some 'Maya Yazbeck' cabaret entertainer.

But it was his grandmother's strong voice that the doctor's reminded him of, even though Nana Gobbo's became screechy with age. He thought he could remember his mother's singing, but he couldn't distinguish it from the singing at her unveiling in the graveyard with its view across the bay. The Maori and the Italian songs, and Uncle Antonio's tear-soaked, drunken baritone out-of-synch with the women dressed in black. That was something like the view he thought he'd been dreaming, but maybe it was just the doctor's singing downstairs that pushed that image into his mind?

At any rate, he was awake and had the sense of a wide-open space, of a song that went out into the sunlit distance. And how bizarre that he associated his own view into that possible future with the scary doctor, not with the intriguing cabaret singer whose reality the doctor had kicked aside with that mixture of sarcasm and disdain. Once, not so long ago, he'd have run salivating after the cabaret singer, *Maya Yazbeck* even sounded hot.

But now, here he was. He'd woken up with his mind reaching out after Hawwa Habash, reaching out to the places where that was *who she was*, not Maya Yazbeck – where he wouldn't be Rosenstein any more, either.

He had indeed fallen asleep in the armchair, and had a nasty taste in his mouth, so he took a swig of the mineral water, then opened the window and the jalousie to spit a mouthful into the street. Looking out, he took a long swallow. It was still dark, and his only watch had been the one in his cellphone, now smashed to bits somewhere along the route the white taxi had taken to get here. He could still remember the sensation of the woman's strong, bony fingers digging the phone out of his jacket pocket, and the brief rush of cool air as she opened the window to chuck it into the street. Perhaps it hadn't broken, and someone had found it, or would in the morning? What would they do? Try the numbers in it? 'Hello? I just found this – on Quai de Lunel. Perhaps you should try to locate the owner?' Yeah, right.

Quai de Lunel was his best guess – seemed like they'd headed for the port – but really, he didn't have a clue. It was mostly quiet outside but he could hear some big trucks manoeuvring somewhere on the other side of the building, and an arterial road of some kind in the middle distance. It couldn't be very long until dawn if the produce was coming in. Probably about 4 a.m. Chefs' hour.

It was chilly with the window open so he closed it and the shutters again, hesitating for a moment over the small lurch in his stomach that told him he was deciding not to scream or jump or anything. And why was that? He reached down to touch his toes, feeling the slightly unyielding obstacle of his stomach, and then did some stretches side to side, running his open palms down the outsides of his trousers, then rotated his head and neck, hearing somehow inside his skull the grinding of cartilage – how did that work?

And why was he sticking with this shit-hole of a place? With the possibility that these people might decide to kill him?

Because he'd chosen it. Because his choice had opened something up, let the possibility of some kind of light in, given him a sense of future. Try explaining that to TG, supposing she'd be interested these days. Or to Bob, the miserable prick. Could he have explained it to his mother, whose peach-fuzz cheek he still remembered, or thought he did? She'd chosen to get pregnant with a shearer called Hare who'd fucked off and left her to it, and then one day she'd chosen to get in a car with a pissed driver and been written off against a bridge along the coast towards Te Kaha – the Kereu River, he went there with the aunties and uncles, the ones with funny Italian names, and Nana Gobbo, they sang and did karakia and a blessing by the chipped concrete of the bridge and took a stone from the river back to Mietta's grave at Tolaga Bay. Then the unveiling – Uncle Antonio throwing himself on the stone.

Did that matter now? Did anything matter from that long ago? It mattered a lot more than what was just outside the window, which was the past that was so close he could still almost return to it if he chose. He could yell and scream, chuck the table or a chair out the window – '*Au secours! Au secours!'* – and get the cops to come, and go back to where he'd left off in the mediocre *cuisine traditionnelle Provençale* restaurant, and even get some good magazine copy out of it, maybe an interview or two . . .

Or not. Or he could go on in the direction that would open up as soon as the door to this room did again. When the rooster-box would be lifted, in the morning, when it would be too late for him to disturb anyone, when no one would pay any attention anyway.

And, despite the squirm of nausea that was really fear in his stomach, he still felt pretty calm – was there any reason to think Doctor Hawwa Habash wasn't intending to put a bullet in his head? There was no good reason why he should believe she didn't plan to do that. But if she'd been serious about it, he'd be dead by now, wouldn't he? In the harbour, probably, with a truck axle or something tied to him. And then there was the way she'd said, *On the contrary. It make very good sense, I understand completely. For me it is also perhaps not so different.*

'It make very good sense,' he said to himself, imitating her slightly odd English. 'It ma-ke . . .'

How did he get here, how did that make sense? Watching the shit the cooks churned out at the back of the Castaway on Oriental Parade, Wellington, the greasy schnitzels that came back with cigarettes stubbed out on them, while he scraped and washed pots, or loaded up the dishwashers with caustic powder. His knife-set when he graduated from cooking school, and the beautiful seven-inch cleaver that Uncle Antonio wrecked by showing off how to sharpen it on Nana's doorstep – which he suspected at the time was a message that he'd better not get too big for his boots.

But the meal he cooked for them all at Tolaga Bay the first time he was going to Italy, after making sous-chef over in Noosa. First the octopus-paste crostini to whet the appetite and get the wine open, then an antipasto of stuffed vegetables, then a silk-handkerchief pasta with pesto sauce, then the fish, crayfish and paua on a bed of peas and potatoes, then the meat of wild pork with *salsa verde* and a big dish of green beans with garlic and anchovies, and finally a rhubarb and ricotta tart.

A couple of the uncles and aunties were gone, his mother too, a long time ago – but Nana Gobbo was still there, she was in her late eighties. She took her teeth out to eat the soft foods, put them back in to deal to the pork, and drank half a glass of wine with each course. At the end she grinned at him with her teeth in, kissed her fingertips, and blinked tears of pride.

Uncle Antonio fell asleep under a shade awning they'd stretched from the clothes-line to the back fence. The rest of them began to sing. The guitars came out, and even a squeeze-box. They sang Dean Martin standards, *Pokarekare Ana*, and Nana Gobbo a screechy song in Italian. One of the distant cousins came on to him and they committed an indiscretion up the back of the orchard. Probably shouldn't have. Sheep were bleating hoarsely and there were late-summer cicadas. He was some kind of local hero.

He was drunk and pleased with himself, and he left the next day with a list of distant Ligurian relatives who might or might not be alive, to catch the bus to Gisborne, and the plane to Auckland, and the next one to Rome, and the train to Genoa. Nana Gobbo gave him a Saint Christopher to hang around his neck. 'Food is love, Christopher. And don't you forget it.' The last time he saw her. Now she was next to his mother, Mietta, with a view of the bay.

What was that supposed to mean, *food is love*?

The recipe-book greed at book-signings. The floor-manager ripping his headphones off and throwing them on the floor at a TV recording session. Cussac screaming at him in Monaco. Bob: 'You've had a good run, Chris.' The arsehole. 'If only you hadn't stuffed handfuls of it down the toilets of the exotic food Meccas with which your brand is now associated.' Or words to that effect.

Food is love – at first his mantra, but in the end his SOS.

He seemed to remember paying his respects at Mietta's grave on the day of his famous lunch, and how his wonderful future had opened out like a view across the bay to pillars of light-filled rain marching across the horizon, and his mother's voice, his uncertain memory of it, singing in that bright, teary space.

But then he also knew, because the memory made him sob, that he couldn't trust it. Because what was it, really, that moved him? That he couldn't remember? Or that he could remember something, but didn't know what it was? Or that the lovely, light-shafted view from the home he felt as though he was now leaving all over again to seek his future fortune was in fact empty? Mietta wasn't there, nor was her voice or even his self-indulgent memory of it. TG wasn't there. What was really filling up the space reserved for memory was his own familiar self-pity.

So when the sound of Hawwa Habash reminded him of his mother singing, could he trust that memory of hope? Or his new sensation of a view of his future opening up again? As it had years ago on the day of his legendary lunch at Tolaga Bay? He hadn't been wrong then – why should he be wrong now? Was it wrong to hope? Was he just being the fool – the *dolt* – that TG mocked but had also loved? Did Hawwa Habash see the fool that TG saw? Or did she see an opportunity in him, something that could be cooked, as she'd said? 'Maybe we cook it?'

This is the only place from which I can go forward. She'd understood that at the same moment he'd astonished himself by saying it. So, maybe.

He just couldn't go past it, the distant sound of the doctor's singing, the intensity of it, some kind of emotion he couldn't tune in to. It reminded him. Not of the actual aunties and uncles starting their repertoire all over again, with slurred gusto, over the ruins of his forever famous lunch, in late summer on the Coast, but a memory of *how he'd remembered it*. How he'd made a point of recalling it, until it became a kind of recording he could put on, with rich effects of summer heat and his tough-girl cousin's practical hand yanking his pants down in the dry grass at the back of the orchard.

Somewhere along the line he'd stopped playing the recording. About the time he'd begun to jeer at the book-signings, probably. About the time TG had begun to ask, 'Where are you, Christopher?'

That's what he'd been reminded of. The sound of the tall, scary doctor harshly singing down there below him in the house reminded him that he'd forgotten to remember the sound of his pissed aunties, uncles and cousins singing 'All of Me', and 'Memories Are Made of This', and 'That's Amore': *When you walk in a dream but you know you're not dreaming, signore.*

The doctor came quickly into the room, closing the door behind her, waving her big hand at him to shut up. He paused, holding the flamboyant Dean Martin pose with one hand on his heart and the other outstretched towards her.

'Please,' she hissed, 'my colleague, the old man, he is sleep.'

Her English was even odder than before, probably because she was flustered, entering the room hastily with a laptop bag over her shoulder and trying to close the door behind her. But also because she was laughing. He couldn't believe it. Doctor Hawwa Habash, who'd poked him in the ribs with a gun, smacked him a good one in the face, and not ruled out the possibility that she might kill him, now had her free hand over her mouth and he could see from the way her eyes were creased up, and hear from her attempts to silence her snorts, that she was in stitches.

'You think this is funny?' he demanded, gesturing at the room, playing the moment for laughs – of course he was kidding, and she could see that. But the moment had passed, as Bob used to say whenever an issue of the magazine missed the fresh beat with a story: he called it 'the moment past'. It passed, and her face, which he noticed looked scrubbed and plain, bare of makeup, had that not-funny look again. Only now she appeared older and almost vulnerable, somewhat exposed even, like someone seen in their dressing gown in early morning, in a cautiously opened doorway.

'No,' she said, 'of course it is not *fun-ny.*' That phrasing she did. 'Mr Hare.' Not looking at him. 'Please to excuse me, my bad manners.'

This could go on, he thought, but best to leave it there.

Was this the moment to ask her, *truthfully*, what was it that he might be able to do – for her, for her work? The question went out into that sensation he had of light and space. An opening-out, the bay, the singing, his dream. A balloon of hope filling his stomach and chest. And fear – that he might now do it. Might now be able to ask the question.

And at the same time, he was afraid he might not be able to. So he sat down.

She unpacked the laptop on the grubby table and put her cellphone next to it. Quickly, with the kind of nimble confidence he'd never even attempted, despite Bob's pleas to get the technology 'under his belt' – how many more hidden barbs would he uncover? – the doctor was getting an internet connection, maybe even a phone one.

He felt a conflict of dread and excitement. Was it possible to call the future? Might TG still be there?

He sat there opposite Dr Habash, waiting.

'Who you gonna call?' he said, knowing she wouldn't get the reference. She was concentrating on her quick actions over the keyboard, and he watched her large and somewhat murky eyes swiftly tracking the results he couldn't see, on the screen. It was his chance to look at her face without her noticing. It had much of what TG somewhat bitchily used to call 'character' – the grand nose, the full, downturned, slightly embittered lips, the prominent eyes. The quality of her attention and the speed of her movements were full of intelligence. Despite the obvious signs of weariness or even exhaustion in her face and posture, she conveyed a sense of powerful, abrasive energy. She reached up to her face with the gesture that he'd become familiar with, and pinched at the dark bag under one eye. She was completing her work on the laptop with one hand, in fact one finger by the sound of it. Then, abruptly, she looked up and caught him staring at her.

The steady hardness of her gaze jolted him – not exactly a slap, but the next best thing. She sure as hell wasn't laughing any more.

'Yes,' she said. 'Who are you going to call? Must be someone who value you?'

He'd been on the verge of riding over the shock of her return glare and saying something like how much he'd have appreciated the chance to get to know her better, and hear more about her work, supposing that had ever been possible, or might yet be possible. He would have meant it, too, because he was in truth quite captivated by the compelling power of the woman, and was sure that under different circumstances she'd be good company, with much to tell him. The kind of person you could imagine spending an evening with, over a good meal perhaps, enjoying the listening, someone who was both serious and, he'd seen, equipped with a sardonic sense of humour.

But now he just felt slapped again, blushing, hot, and his face must have shown the heat, because she repeated her question, flatly, awkwardly recalibrating her language.

'We contact someone who have for you a value.' She clicked her tongue in frustration. 'Somebody who need to restore you.' She was looking at him closely, shaking her head at her own question. 'You understand what I am saying, Mr Hare?' The pause. 'Christopher?'

'Oh, so it's *Christopher* again, is it?' Some of his spit landed on the lid of the laptop.

'Excuse me?'

'Now that we're finally down to it. Cut-the-crap time.'

She sat back somewhat carefully with her hands on the armrests of the chair. He could see the weight of the gun in her jacket pocket.

He made a derisive gun with two fingers of his right hand and fired it into his head. 'For fuck's sake. Do you really think I'm going to try something?'

'I am asking if there is somebody you like to contact. Why this makes you angry?'

'We're talking about hostage money, aren't we. My *value*?' He was trembling again, after having been calm for so long. The fluttering sensation in his chest. 'Somebody to *restore* me, did you say? You could have spared me the waiting.' His disappointment – his *grief* – was choking him.

He saw her get it – at first a look of disbelief. Then the hand to her mouth, a chesty bark of laughter.

'Yes, of course, excuse me, this is what we do, Arabs, especially Palestinians, we hostage a famous food writer, you are right, I should have explain. This is what we always do.' She was really enjoying herself. 'You hear perhaps what happen to that famous restaurant at Biarritz, it gets bombed. What we do with cooking when,' she spoke the phrase with ironic care as if quoting a news report, '*our demands are not met*.'

Yes, he knew about that one. It was another of Ducasse's. Some kind of resort. Ducasse had had to shut it down.

'That was Basques,' he said. 'Not Arabs. What are you talking about?' Clearly, he'd got it wrong. This wasn't about ransoming him. Not that he was about to apologise.

The woman passed a hand over her eyes and muttered something in French. He caught the word *imbécile*.

'Oh yes,' he said. 'You must think I'm pretty stupid. What I did. But what do you expect? You could have just let me go.'

'No – you are not stupid. To the contrary. When I say "*imbécile*", I describe myself. Now I will be clear. Before I ask you what you would like to do, who you like to contact. Not to talk, it's too dangerous. But to leave a message. For example, like here.'

She turned the laptop towards him and, leaning in, he next jumped back at the sight of an image of TG. It was her website. There she was, Mary Pepper, Pepper herself, the one and only, that wisp of hair. He could clearly imagine her little head-flick, to get it away from her eyebrow. She was standing in front of one of her huge, 150 x 200 cm photographs, this one with vague towering shapes, yellow and tan, maybe gourds.

That cool Pepper smile.

'Please,' said Hawwa Habash. 'Do not upset yourself. I know that this is your wife, an artist. Before you don't like to mention her. But now we have little time. Your relationship is not my business. But please. I think you should send a message to this woman. She is what I can find. I find her before, not hard. Often you are together when I Google. Now we can do it, it's simple.' She hesitated, her lips pursed as if considering a diagnosis or something doctorish – looking at him carefully, thinking. 'Then, after a while, perhaps you can go.'

'I can go?' He couldn't believe it.

'Perhaps. In a while. I think so.'

Where would he go? This was the first thought that entered his head, which was ringing slightly as if from a loud noise. He'd imagined that the day he'd see when he was turned loose would have Dr Habash in it – he ran out, crowing.

'But where are *you* going?'

The woman's look of incredulity was quickly replaced by one of annoyance, then her familiar stonewall expression.

'Please,' she said curtly, gesturing at the laptop with the image of TG on its screen, 'something for your wife. On her *contact*.' She grimaced as if at a distasteful word. 'We have not very much time.' She turned the laptop back towards herself and held her hands over its keyboard.

'But what do you expect me to say? *Having a great time, wish you were here?*' He didn't get it.

She didn't lift her head, or snap at him this time. Her gaze was downward, her large eyelids blinking rapidly.

'I think maybe you should tell her where you are. If she don't know.'

'What if she doesn't care?'

Then she did lift her face towards him. She looked like a doctor at that moment, he thought: her expression calm and attentive, as if she was explaining something frightening to a patient.

'Please,' she said softly. 'I think you should do this.'

'But you said I could go. So what's the point?'

Still, that doctor's look. He guessed she was offering him something, a warning – they were going to lock him up? But that wasn't what she'd said. *You can go. Perhaps. In a while.* And anyway, he'd decided.

'Okay, what the hell. So where am I, for a start?'

'That, I will write. From you, just a message. Something . . . *intime*. For her.'

'Food is love.'

She hesitated, as if not believing him, or that she'd not heard correctly. Her doctor's look replaced by the derisive one.

'She'll know what it means. Who it's from.'

'*Food-is-love*.' She typed, making the shapes of the words with her scornful lips. 'But still I have to say it is from you. From her hus-band. From *Christopher*. Otherwise she will reject.' She shot him a look. He could see that she was guessing quite a lot, but not really interested. 'And that is all?'

When he didn't respond, she unleashed a curt flurry of keyboard-taps and then closed the laptop. A strange silence. That direct look of hers, her heavy eyelids going up and down.

'It was what my grandmother used to say, *Food is love*.' He felt he should explain – hesitating only because he'd become accustomed to the doctor's impatience. But this time she waited, politely, as if they'd entered the space of conversation she'd mocked last time they talked. 'She was from Italy, around Chiavari in Liguria. She came to New Zealand after the war, with my grandfather. He was Maori. She was my first teacher. Of cooking. And Italian.'

'But why you send this to your wife? This speech of your grandmother?'

He had the feeling that she was thinking about her next move, having been so busy with him before. But her face was calm and tired, not haughty, as if something had resolved itself during the business with the laptop.

'Because I told her this story at the beginning. The story of my grandmother's saying. When we . . .'

'When you fall in love with her, I think.'

He was astonished – Doctor Hawwa Habash was smiling at him, without mockery, even with weary sentimentality.

'Yes, although I didn't tell her that part until later. But I knew. It was our first assignment, you know what that means? *Notre mission*. I was the writer, she was the photographer. We had a meal – in Paris.'

The doctor's 'Ah' was quiet, and a furrow appeared between her eyes.

'My grandmother also used to say, "Who can cook and not drink the cooking wine?"' He was watching the look of unease on the woman's face. What was he saying that might be bothering her? He blundered on. '"Who can eat and not make love to the cook?"'

'Where I come from, the Bedouin say, "The woman died of exhaustion and the *mansaf* lasted but a day." *My* grandmother used to say it.' Her contribution was somewhat perfunctory. She seemed about to leave, or to move on – that 'moment past' sensation again. But he wanted her to stay a little longer, in the room but also in the moment, in this conversation. He so badly wanted her to stay in this present, after which he'd probably never see her again, however much he imagined *leaving* towards a future she'd made possible; a future in which, perhaps, they could work together. With the children, with food. They'd never be in this situation again, on the very edge of whatever was going to happen next. So he went on talking towards her by-now-formal smile, whose politeness he could see was in preparation for whatever she had planned next, which might be her departure, since she was packing up her laptop.

'That meal, that *food is love* one, it was at a restaurant in Paris called Le Baratin, a little one, Argentinian, twentieth arrondissement, that's when it happened. That I fell in love with her. Boy, did I ever. Boom!' He clutched his heart and was going to continue, just babbling really, to keep the moment, to stall another of her abrupt, efficient exits. But her face had suddenly gone a pale khaki colour and she made a guttural 'Uh!' sound in her chest. She looked sick, as if she might be going to faint.

'Le Baratin, *tamam*!' Her voice hoarse, the angry foreign word drawn out in a groan.

'You know it?' How stupid that sounded, when she looked as though she'd seen a ghost.

Her hands had flown to her cheeks, as if holding her face together. 'Yes, I know this place. Maybe twenty years ago, we often go there. It just open, Le Baratin. On rue Jouye-Rouve, yes? We live near there.'

'We?' He'd seen how she immediately stopped herself. 'Don't tell me you also fell in love at Le Baratin! Now that *would* be bizarre.'

'Yes, *bizarre*, as you say, like a mad dog.'

Whatever that meant. But now she was the hard Hawwa Habash again. Outside in the distance a police siren started up and sped away. They watched each other noticing it.

She awarded him a grim smile. 'No, not coming here. If the police come here they do not make a noise.'

Then she moved the laptop case aside and leaned forward, as close to him as she could get across the table. He could smell aniseed on her breath. She spoke urgently, as if the siren had reminded her that time was running out.

'That man in the restaurant, that I shoot. He was my husband. Now you have to know this. But yes, we also are in love at Le Baratin. Or I think we are. Then, I think we are.' She shrugged. 'I was young.'

He couldn't think of anything to say.

'Now I have begun to answer your question. Why did I do it? Now I will tell you.'

'No,' he said. 'Please. It doesn't matter. I don't have to know. I don't even want to.'

'But when you jump in the car with me, what do you do? You think it was empty? This place from where, as you say, you can *go forward*? You can just jump in and then jump out again?'

He stood up from his chair to avoid the hiss of her scorn, and began to walk around the room, but she continued, following him with her harsh voice, snapping the words out at the front of her mouth – one after the other, the shit her husband had done. Arms deals, ripping off medical supplies, stealing aid money, trafficking kidneys, 'adoptions'. He really didn't want to know – if he got out of here, this stuff would surely put a bullet in his head.

'Please,' he begged. 'Please. I really don't want to know.'

'But, Christopher, now you do. Now you know it.'

'What's that supposed to mean?'

'And even the Gucci bag,' she said. 'The one you put your head in.'

'*I* put my head in? I like that!'

'Was meant to be left behind. As a message to the associates of my husband. Was a fake, from New Jersey. That my husband imports. But then you return it. Like a good dog. But this bag – shall we say it was full of what I tell you. Much information. And now you have it, when you leave this place, *the only one from which you can go forward*, as you say yourself.'

'What do you expect me to do with all this?' But he knew the answer. He'd started to know it when he ran out of the restaurant and jumped into the white taxi.

'My husband that I shoot was for a long time a criminal and a murderer – now I know this, but then, at Le Baratin, maybe I choose not to know. So now I have to be responsible for this. For my choosing not to know. And also for the death of my son.'

Now she stood up and pursued him to the far side of the room, by the window. Aniseed breath, one strong hand on his arm. 'His name was Boutros. He was seven years old. We go to Beirut, everybody believes the war is finished finally. He has grown up in Paris and in Amman after the *fedayeen* have gone. He has never heard the sound of guns, of bombing. When the Syrians attack Aoun he went to the roof to see it, though I have forbidden him. So someone shoot him. Maybe they think he is a sniper, maybe just an accident. But also because Boutros does not understand danger.'

'I'm very sorry,' he said.

'Yes, I believe you. But now, also, you understand what I am trying to say. That there was much danger in the bag you decide to pick up. So you will be responsible for what happen next.'

'You're on your own, kid.'

She grimaced. 'If you like.'

'But I can go.'

'As you choose.'

'But not with you.'

She didn't bother to answer. He sensed that she'd expected more of him. But what?

'Perhaps you would like to sleep. Until daytime.'

'I can't go now?'

'There is a bed. I show you.'

'That's a no?'

She picked up the laptop bag and cellphone and took those long strides to the door. Opened it and jerked her head at him. That 'moment past' feeling.

There was a single bed in the room she showed him, across the landing from the one they'd been in. It was covered with a plaid blanket. She picked up a small elegant cabin bag and a dark overcoat and stood in the doorway with the laptop valise over her shoulder. Then he got it – she and the others were going to leave first, without him.

'Goodbye, Mr Hare,' she said.

'Christopher,' he said. 'You can call me Christopher.' He felt absurdly sad.

'Yes – Christopher.' She seemed to hesitate a moment. But then she abruptly closed the door. The lock clicked over.

He stood there wondering what else he could have said. Then he turned the light out and lay down on the bed. There was nothing else to do. The shutters were open and the city's distant rumble of chefs'-hour activity entered the room in which he could smell traces of the doctor's perfume. On the pillow, too, something astringent, pricey – and, he thought, perhaps a hint of garlic. And the vague imprint of what might have been lipstick.

He lay there with his cheek pressed to the pillow, inhaling the faint, bracing bouquet of Hawwa Habash. It was the confusing aroma of a human being. He remembered a grinning vintner in the marketplace of Malaucène in the Ventoux who'd had the ability to close one nostril of the huge beaky nose he lowered into his glass. He tried doing that: inhaling Habash, to pass the time, never imagining he could fall asleep, not with his mind opening and shutting on a future that seemed possible at one moment and impossible the next.

CHAPTER 8

What on earth was she supposed to do with this wretched 'food is love' message popping up via her website? And this address in Nice? Bob was looking at her sternly. He kept her at arm's length these days, but who else could she turn to?

'Have you heard from the silly man, Bob?'

What had Christopher got himself into? And what about this Maya Yazbeck? If nothing else, she sounded exotic. Was the prick gloating?

That little pang of jealousy, so stupid.

'Out of the kindness of my heart – truly, Mary, because I love the fool – I gave him the off-season gig. For old time's sake. He was broke of course. I told him, seek out the little-known bargains, the ones that don't fleece tourists. What he used to be good at.'

'You mean the ones that can't get any tourists, even in summer.'

Once, Bob had thought she was the cat's pyjamas. Now, as far as he was concerned, she was an ungrateful bitch. But what did he expect? That she'd go on forever being Thé Glacé? Trotting around in lockstep with the husband he'd practically pimped her to, however hard he'd tried to play outraged later on?

He wasn't exactly glaring at her, he was probably still quite fond of her deep down. Once he got over his sense of betrayal. But he was going to show her the door soon, if she didn't stop being snippy.

'Sorry, sorry, sorry, I'm sorry Bob. You were always my life-saver. Always will be. But he's such a moody old fool, our Christopher.'

Food is love, for God's sake. Of course she still remembered Christopher's gorgeous tipsy face leaning across the table at Le Baratin. His eyes shining as if with the same *joues de boeuf* juices that he wiped from those grinning lips, before he reached across to raid her plate.

But that was then.

Bob was fussing about with a file of clippings and print-outs. It was completely miserable outside. Everything the colour of pencil-lead, rain with a bit of late season's hail plinking at the window. The kind of day when Christopher could get moody. But also the kind of day when he used to make staying in bed with a late breakfast irresistible.

Up to a point. His dreadful attempts at funny translated curses.

'I spit on the milk of your mother's work-schedule!'

'For God's sake, Christopher, shut up, stop being boring and horrible. They'll come for you.'

'Who – who will come for me? Will you come for me, Pepper?'

So dreadful. Just desperate, sometimes.

Bob gave her a sheet of paper with addresses circled in red biro.

'Darling, don't go getting tangled up with all that again. The man's a tarpit. If you don't mind me saying so. You know how I loathe your ghastly new work, but I do still adore you.'

He reached over his desk and put the hand-of-compassion on the one with which she held the print-out. 'He was good for you. I even take some credit for that. But let him go, treasure. It'll end in tears again.'

'I'll tell you what's peculiar, Bob.' Or perhaps not now. She saw him flinch at the prospect of their chat going on much longer.

How was he to know she'd been up half the night thinking about it, that 'food is love'? Why it sounded so wrong – off-key, mistimed, out-of-place, clumsy even for Christopher. And the wretched parade of memories it brought plodding through her mind. Food, sex, charm, fun, blah blah blah.

She couldn't work, couldn't put her mind to anything that didn't recall some absurd image of Christopher. For example, him eating a dripping pistachio gelato in Nice, on that first trip. The original catastrophe. Opening up his shirt so the sticky green drips could miss it and just land on his stupid fuzzy chest.

Yes, she'd so wanted to lick the icecream *off* him. Right there. Before they'd even screwed for the first time, on the train.

But did she have to be reminded?

'Where did *you* go, dear?' Bob's patience wearing thin.

'What's peculiar – I probably shouldn't have, Bob, you'll scold me. But I replied to this person's message, this Maya Yazbeck@hotmail.com. I said *What is this, a joke?*'

'What do you mean, "person"? Didn't I hear you say *woman* before?' Getting his spank in. He fetched the open bottle of Rhône *villages*. Half with lunch and half later in the afternoon.

Dinner required another class of drink, for Bob.

Now was later in the afternoon, she thought, and couldn't stop it. Partly, she was just so tired. She began to cry after the first swallow, feebly, because maybe Christopher had got himself into one of his moods. And done something really stupid this time.

Even though she couldn't bear him.

'I tried to reply to this person's email, and it just bounced. No such address.' She blew her nose into a tissue from the box Bob put in front of her. She knew how much he hated crying. So did she. A big swallow of the nice kind wine. Another one. 'Don't you think that's . . . sinister?'

She'd handed Bob this one on a plate.

'Could have been someone who doesn't like your work. You know, one of those cranks – people who love food?'

'Come off it, Bob – "food is love"? It was him.'

'*That* could have been a coincidence. Admit it.'

She wouldn't be provoked. 'Then I thought, why not? Why not try? I Googled Maya Yazbeck. There was only one obvious person. A Lebanese cabaret *artiste* for God's sake. What kind of singer writes *food is love*?'

'A starving one.'

She talked on over the top of Bob's sniggering.

'And it *was* a woman. Why did that not surprise me, Bob? Then I looked up Maya, it means princess in Arabic.'

Bob drank.

'Proves without doubt that she was a woman, Bob. Is. Princesses are.'

'Imagine this,' drawled Bob. He was trying but failing to soothe her, with his droll, late-afternoon manner, which she could see all the way through. Or perhaps he was trying to provoke her again. 'Christopher Hare meets an exotic Lebanese singer in an out-of-season dump somewhere off the beaten track in Nice and decides to taunt his ex-wife with a provocative message.' He raised his glass. 'Sounds like our man.'

She nearly threw her wine in his smug face.

'Sorry,' he said. 'That wasn't very funny.'

'No, not funny, and not fair either. That was horrible. You know Christopher, he's a hopeless, self-centred cry-baby, but no malice, Bob. None at all. Unlike most of the people in this wretched city.'

She looked at the piece of paper Bob had given her. 'What's this?'

Bob's nasty jibe was replaying in her head.

'Christopher's draft schedule. For the off-season issue. For his trip. No point giving him more than a draft, he'll never stick to it. But it might give you some idea of where he was.' He corrected. 'Is.' Again. 'Could be. He's supposed to be in Nice now.'

'The Yazbeck I found on Google is a top Lebanese singer based in Beirut. With an international following of men with gold chains. What's she doing in Nice in the off-season? For that matter, why would she send me a street address? It stinks, Bob.'

Now Bob was looking slightly interested. He refilled them.

'I'm telling you, Christopher would run a mile. This is one thoroughbred camel. What on earth would they find to talk about? If he could get past the bodyguards.'

'Well, then, it wasn't her. He's pulling your leg.'

'But if it wasn't her, that's even odder. For example, why was he using her email? And why wouldn't her email work when I tried to reply?'

Bob was getting bored. 'Odd is what you get with Christopher. You know that. It's what he does. *Passé,* but terribly hard to miss.'

Now he was being vengeful. Frowning his big eyebrows. He pushed the cork back into the bottle without topping her up.

She couldn't help noticing one of her photographs framed on the wall, and the three books she'd done with Christopher stacked tidily on the coffee table. Along with Christopher's guide to Italian wines.

Oh, they'd been an asset, Christopher Hare and Mary Pepper. The photograph was of the *mansaf* they'd been treated to in Wadi Rum in Jordan. Without the sheep's head, for the benefit of delicate readers.

A circle of swarthy wrists and hands reaching in toward the food, some with expensive wristwatches on them. There was Christopher's paler hand, with the wedding ring on it.

'I'll tell you what was really odd.'

But it was too late. Bob had had enough. Enough of her

and enough of Christopher. Christopher was washed up, and she was making pictures Bob loathed.

She finished her glass and accepted his perfunctory pecks on both cheeks. Lovely to see her, she didn't think so, not really.

'Tell me when you find out what this is all about, Mary. Check the review schedule. There was one in Nice. Maybe they do an exotic floor show?' Bob's weary expression said he didn't know or care.

'No, you tell me when you hear from him, Bob. When he gets back. He doesn't talk to me any more.'

In the South Kensington underground there was a billboard advertising her next exhibition. She looked at it through the gaps between people standing four-deep on the rush-hour platform. She was going to be showing at White Cube. 'Mary Pepper: Idyll – New Photographs.'

There she was, very thin and pale in front of huge prints of outsize phallic gourds. 'Mary Pepper keeps it simple', one critic had written. She'd taken it as a compliment.

A young woman with earphones was uttering uncanny, off-key fragments of the song she was listening to, staring at the billboard with a look of blank bliss on her face.

The celebrity Mary Pepper pushed her way back up to the exit and caught a taxi instead. The driver seemed to recognise her.

'Haven't I seen you, Miss?'

'Sorry, I don't want to talk. No offence.'

'Please yourself, Miss.'

She put her earphones in and listened to Franz Ferdinand being rather wet. It made a change.

There was an odd smell of cloves in the cab, quite nice. She thought it might come from the driver's skin, rather sexy. She rebuked the thought.

But then she couldn't help it. The image of the gorgeous, sultry-looking Lebanese singer kept coming back. Along with unworthy, jealous thoughts about her aromas. The ones that changed with body temperature, mood, bathing.

Oh, please, how could she be jealous? Christopher was gone. She was glad.

The day he'd left the flat, he hardly took anything. He didn't want any useful things like sheets. He stuffed his clothes into a suitcase and his laptop into a rucksack with about three books. His toiletries in a Sainsbury's plastic bag. He threw it all into the back of a taxi and climbed in.

From the upstairs bedroom window she saw one ridiculous long leg retract into the taxi and then shoot out again. He seemed to be grappling with something. Probably at least one of the bags had burst open. Then he got his leg inside and slammed the door.

Later, she found odd socks under the bed and threw them out. There were two little brown Moleskine notebooks down the back of the sofa. She posted them to Bob.

She didn't know where he'd gone. Didn't want to, didn't care.

He'd left all his cooking gear except the knives.

'You really expect me to lug this around, Pepper?' A great big paella pan, a couscous steamer, a glazed brown *tajine* pot.

Not that she ever cooked.

A few months later, he sent her a card with one of her own photographs on it, from an exhibition of her work that he'd seen while in Tokyo. She didn't believe him. Not the part about being in Tokyo, but the words of congratulation on the card.

'Saw your show. Stunning!'

He'd have hated it. The lying toad.

Then he stopped contacting her. She heard the salacious gossip about women and ignored it.

What was really odd about this email from the latest one, the part that would have shut Bob up, was the subject line. It read, 'Message from your husband Christopher Hare'.

Christopher hadn't written that – never, never, never – he just wouldn't. Not even if he was playing with her. And he didn't do that anymore. He hadn't since their row over her first exhibition. Two years ago. And if he hadn't sent it, then that fucking Lebanese cunt must have. And why did she need a message from her 'husband Christopher Hare'?

Over and over.

When she got out at her flat she gave the taxi-driver a big tip, to apologise for her rudeness.

'Good luck with the exhibition, Miss,' he said. 'I'm an artist myself. Got to make ends meet, don't we?'

Maybe they could have had a nice chat on the way home about her time taking photographs of table settings. Ten years. And subsequently, after meeting up with Christopher Hare, of food that exemplified the maxim, if you can't eat it fuck it.

About another ten.

'Sorry, Miss,' said the taxi driver, shutting his smile down. 'No offense. You enjoy yourself now. You be sure to do thaa-at.'

As he drove off he gave her a fuck-you two-finger salute out the window. She deserved it. What a miserable cunt she was turning into.

There was a message from Bob on her home phone. 'Mary – phone me. Or turn your mobile on.' But she couldn't be bothered with one of his drunken apologies. She'd ring him in the morning when he'd had time to get over it.

She poured herself a large glass of wine and watched the Channel 4 news. Jon Snow was tearing strips off someone. He'd interviewed Christopher once. He'd been terrific, Christopher had. He'd made Snow laugh with a puerile joke about curry and farting.

The phone rang again but she let the machine answer it. Probably Bob again, begging her to phone him so he could feel better. He'd have broached a new bottle by now.

No, she couldn't. Phone him.

She was sick of all this. He'd practically kicked her out.

She got her bag and found Christopher's schedule. She knew it was going to make her feel sad, and it did.

She put on a CD: Michel Legrand playing Eric Satie's *Gymnopédies*.

Who was she kidding? Want to get miserable, go all the way.

She took it off, and put on Gram Parsons & the Fallen Angels. Live, with Emmylou Harris. 'We'll Sweep Out the Ashes': *I didn't mean to start this fire and neither did you.*

Christopher's last schedule, his swan song. These were places they'd been. The narrow band of cheap rail links and budget flights. This time, Paris, Lyon, and Marseille, and he should be in Nice, so the email had probably come from Nice. Unless he'd changed the schedule.

Which was likely, knowing Christopher. Off on some tangent. For example, back to Genoa. For the *Cappon Magro*.

Then he was going to a budget ski-resort in the Alpes-Maritimes, at Limone, over the Italian border. What in God's name was he supposed to do there?

She laughed at the thought of Christopher in his baggy clothes at a ski resort. His shirt hanging out, his scuffed on-the-road Blundstone boots. Picking his way through a plate of small mountain trout. Making them *be* something, or crash into each other.

Without her there, so he couldn't say, 'Look, Pepper – a trout-wreck!'

While hearty, tanned skiers replenished themselves and boasted.

And then what was he going to do?

She pictured him getting on the bus to the airport at Nice. In a small polite queue outside the *gare routière*. He'd be charming someone or other with his fluent but peculiar French. There was bound to be laughter.

Then, in her mind, he just seemed to evaporate.

And of course, now the Fallen Angels were singing *Love is like a stove, burns you when it's hot.*

It was the end of the road, for Christopher, with Bob and the magazine. The books had gone off the boil. And anyway she wasn't 'available' to do the photographs. The television show had been canned, total disaster, he was history there. Likewise the summer schools in Provence. Self-destruction as an art form.

He'd probably go back to cooking. Maybe he'd even go back to New Zealand. He'd be all right. Someone would always adore him.

'Six Days on the Road': *Gonna make it home tonight* . . . Emmylou and Gram winding around each other like a couple of snakes.

But love the fool or not, admit it: the world would be a *drearier* place without those mouth-watering columns.

They'd woken her up again to *sensation* all those years ago when she also heard the little family living its life in the flat below. They were so in the moment. Ska music and the lovely young daddy trumpeting like an elephant. The little girl laughing and consenting to eat her dinner.

The next glass of wine made her feel maudlin and rebellious.

Emmylou and Gram had gone treacly. Also a bit smack-dreamy and drawly.

Time for Miles and Coltrane, 'Straight, No Chaser.'

In Nice, the restaurant he'd been assigned to review was called Le Lapin Sauvage. Now that was original. She could just picture it, cheerful tablecloths. There was a phone number. She'd telephone them in the morning, and then Bob.

Those Ligurian dishes he loved best, his grandmother's. Each name a little song.

Vellutata di porri.

Zuppa di primavera.

Christopher's appalling Dean Martin routine. *That's amore!*

She should eat something.

Food is love.

That was then.

But where was now? She wanted it to be where she was. She wanted to be where it was. *Me, myself, here, now*, the title of some artist's show, unforgettable. But it wasn't, she wasn't. She was never completely just *here, now.* Nearly, when Danny pushed down the hypo plunger and a cocoon of the present ballooned around her. But that was vague and muffled.

Other times, undeniably, with Christopher. Sensational. Unbearable, in the end. But sensational, *here, now.* Sometimes.

These days *here, now* happened when she was taking photographs – but only sometimes.

Miles and Coltrane, 'Two Bass Hit.' The two of them so utterly together in it.

In the moment. At the present time. All those phrases, they were so full of longing. But when she looked at what she'd done in the moment, in the present moment, at the photograph of the moment, she wasn't ever there.

Only the ghost of her, a memory of the sensation of *her.*

What she'd meant.

What she'd meant by the photograph of the *mansaf* Bob had on the wall of his office. Which was also the reason she and Christopher fought over it.

'What do you like about this one, Christopher?' Picking their way through book illustration options on her big monitor. He was bored and fidgety. He kept making annoying clicky, whistly noises with his lips, smothering yawns.

'I like it because . . .' Really, he just wanted to move on.

To finish the job, to let her decide. 'I like it because it looks like a whole lot of food, Pepper. Which it was – remember? A *whole* lot.'

'What about the hands?'

He heard her tone. 'What about them, creampuff?'

That was when she lost patience. 'The *whole lot* of food was being eaten, Christopher. By people. That's what was happening – see, the hands?'

'That's what food's all about, treasure.'

'Doesn't it strike you as interesting that the hands aren't attached to anyone?'

'Mine was – it was attached to me.'

Off they went. Boom.

She gave up and left him staring moodily at the screen. Fiddling with his sticking-out bottom lip.

'Fuck you, Christopher, you're so wet. *You* decide. Why don't you choose the whole lot all by your fucking self.'

Because couldn't he see, didn't he even remember? That it wasn't just a *whole lot* of food on the vast table-sized platter on the carpeted floor of the Bedouin tent? It was a *whole lot* of food being eaten by a *whole lot* of men. Who'd been invited to be there. It was about the men who were there more than the food.

They were all men apart from *the photographer*.

They were bigwig Jordanian politicians and businessmen. With bigwig smiles and wristwatches. They were bigwig tourism men.

They were, apparently, local Bedouin sheikhs from Wadi Rum, their hosts that night, looking to improve their tourism revenues with a book by the famous *food writer*. An article in the prestigious *food magazine*. A feature in the *in-flight magazine*.

A TV special on the *mansaf*. With spectacular, irresistible *photographs*.

Eat! Eat more!

This was a safe destination, they insisted. It was completely secure, the troubles were over. Safer than Israel! The heritage, the authenticity, the history, the hospitality. You will definitely want to come back! Everybody does!

She'd been hearing it all day.

And yes, the food was stupendous. Rich yoghurty lamb; rice, almonds, pine nuts, flat bread. The tender cheeks and lips of the sheep's head were removed from the skull and spread across the dish. The skull, and what was left on it, taken away on a plate.

She was offered some of the best bits and yes, they were indescribably delicious.

She thought there were some jokes about testicles hidden in the dish, but the men were too polite to include her.

A fleeting thought about *kashrut* and the non-kosher mixing of meat and dairy. But only fleeting.

Christopher had learned an Arabic word, *mabrouk*. It meant something like 'congratulations'. He kept saying it to loud applause. In return his appetite was being applauded.

So when she excused herself and stood up to take some photographs, she did actually have a plan in mind. The huge, sumptuous dish of delicious food, yes, but also the disembodied hands and wrists. Men's hands, with expensive gold wristwatches.

And her husband's hand among them, the *food writer's* hand. Reaching in, with gusto, *mabrouk*!

Not her hand, the woman's hand, the *photographer's* hand. That was only normal, under the circumstances. She was doing her job, they were eating, the spectacular dish of food had to be photographed. And, before that, of course, it had had to be cooked.

But, leaving hers aside, there were no other women's hands there, reaching in to the dish. The cook's hands weren't there. There were no children's hands, either. She could hear them outside the tent, the women and children, laughing and scolding, and sometimes she could tell that children were peeping under the wall of the tent at the men and their big feast.

Mabrouk, mabrouk!

Outside, it was chilly, though the day had been blisteringly hot. The smell of the heat still rose up from the ground, dusty and aromatic, with tangs of animal shit and kerosene. The sky was dark and clear with a glittering scatter of stars. The daylight pinks and mauves of the sand and buttes were now thick, soft fields and looming piles of deep textured shadow. Even with no moon, the horizon was sharply defined, a black edge of high rock against dark, luminous blue. The stars there seemed to hang *in* space, not against it – the space went back, beyond them. There was a line of white SUVs parked nearby, and the drivers' cigarettes glowed here and there in the dark. A car radio was on, playing a woman's voice winding and winding around some repeated phrases. Some of the drivers were joining in.

Ya habi . . . ii . . . bi!

She'd never been anywhere as beautiful. She didn't want to go back into the tent with the men and the huge *mansaf.*

When she stepped away from it into the darkness she seemed to be stepping away from herself, *the photographer.*

Out of the picture entirely.

I didn't have a hand in it.

This was the quip she'd used for Christopher, the first time they looked at the photographs. Keeping it light. He'd looked at her uneasily, sensing something. But really, that was when she began to step away from him as well.

He'd stopped cheesily singing 'That's *amore*!' The kinds of things he used to do. Months and months ago.

The Ligurian dishes that were like songs his grandmother might have sung.

Mandilli de saea al pesto.

Where did you go, Christopher?

Christopher Where?

When she left the room, back in London, that time they had their seriously big row about the photograph of the *mansaf* – that was when he knew it. That she was leaving him. She could see that he felt her go.

It was the way he sat there, pulling at his stuck-out bottom lip, his face pale and sad in the glow from the screen of tile-sized images of turmeric-coloured chickpeas, purple aubergine skins blackened by hot charcoal, little skewers of minced lamb, plates of sliced tomatoes, red onions and green peppers, a grilled half-chicken dusted with paprika, fried eggs on a bed of seared mint, pale couscous scattered with parsley, a plate of grilled sardines with vivid lemon wedges, a bowl of shining black olives, a shallow dish of *hummus* with oil, olives and paprika on the surface, hard-boiled eggs on blistered pita bread dusted with *za'atar*, a plate of *falafel* dribbled with yoghurt, a *tajine* of carrots with raisins and almonds, a plate of dates, a plate of prunes, glasses of mint tea, a plate of *halva*.

An immense dish of *mansaf* with hands reaching into it, including his, Christopher's.

But not TG's. Not Thé Glacé's.

She no longer had a hand in it.

Now she was quite drunk, and the phone had rung again, more than once. Too late to eat anything and anyway she wasn't hungry.

Pesce al cartoccio.

Seppie in zimino.

Carciofi all'inferno.

The memory of Christopher's dejected hunched shape in front of the computer screen with its *1,001 Nights* pictures was a sad one. But then so was her memory of their final showdown, spectacularly in public, at the opening of her exhibition.

'*Why didn't you tell me?*'

T.G.? Pepper? My *paciugo*? Sweet tooth? Why didn't you?

She had. He should have seen it coming.

So why couldn't he just have said something wonderful and meant it? 'Brilliant! Brilliant!' with that gorgeous smile of his.

Instead, a look of utter horror.

What did he expect?

This was what she knew: that she could be free sometimes, but not often happy. Or happy sometimes, but not often free.

And the man who'd made her happiest? Who'd most often had a hand in her happiness?

Fagiolini all'aglio e acciughe.

The ludicrous stripe of sunshine across his big funny body, and his blubbering mouth saying, 'What am I supposed to do with this *feeling*!' Beating his breast!

When had he stopped singing?

She got up and walked very carefully to the phone to ring Bob, knowing she had to. Of course she had to.

She opened another wine instead.

Put on Joy Division. Ian Curtis singing 'Love Will Tear Us Apart'.

Turned it right up.

CHAPTER 9

'I can go?'

This was what the food writer had said – Christopher. But she had heard in his voice no timbre of urgency, of desire, of impatience. *I can go?* There was even something strange in his articulation, which was at once a statement of his decision and also a question as to his freedom.

Well, that was for him to decide. This was not a stupid man – indeed, inside his comedy, there was an intelligent instinct, a certain intellectual heat. She had watched him understand where he was, now, in the present, in the place from which he could go forward.

She had seen the question attending in his hands and face – *But where, how?* And the speculation in how he looked at her. Clearly this was sad, but of course without doubt the decision had to be his. This was the moment at which she, the doctor, had learned to remove herself from the matter of life and death. Now, he could choose to decide, or choose to let fate decide, but in any case now the choice was his to make, not hers.

In the room downstairs she took the laptop from its satchel and placed it on the table. On top of its closed lid, her long fingers counted and thus removed from her thoughts the tasks she had completed. There remained one.

In thinking about it, she considered the procession of images whose truth had been the narrative of her life, its measure, her authenticity. There was the image of the white-stone house on a small rise in Lydda, with an old grape vine whose trunk was the circumference of an unmarried girl's waist. There was an image like a faded photograph of a long line of people carrying possessions down a road glaring with pale heat, with the short shadows of noon at their feet and a tumbled wall of white stones fencing them in. There was her grandmother wearing a headscarf of Nazareth lace figured with birds and flowers, standing on the rooftop of the house on Jebel Ashrafieh and lifting her hands towards the bellicose sunset. There were the faces of the young *fedayeen* on Jebel Amman, bright with exultant power, parting before her as she ran with Habib through the hot mass of them. The image of children whose phosphorus burns could not be extinguished, who continued to burn in Barbir Hospital after they had died, who burst into flames in the mortuary. The image of Boutros on the roof of the apartment block in Beirut, with one leg bent under him in a way that told her he must be dead. Her husband Abdul Yassou's wide silent grin of fear as she felt the revolver kick back against the heel of her right hand, the one with which she was accustomed to hold the instruments of her healing profession.

Some of these images and many others were in her mind because she had put them there or because the stories she had been told had imprinted them there, and some were there because she had seen the events that the images remembered on her behalf. But they were all within her, and when she moved in time or to a different place they also moved; they would always be there, within her, her substance. She was not distinct from them, indeed they were who she had become during her life, Hawwa Habash, and they and she would now *go forward* free of that false present that had weighed her down for so long.

Now there remained one task, a small one, which would separate her and the images that were the narrative of her life from *this* place and *this* moment, and from the imploring expression on Christopher's face, and from his question that was not entirely a question, 'I can go?'

Yes, she, Hawwa Habash could go now, she could decide to do this, it was simple, and as for the food writer who would surely not be sleeping on the hard bed upstairs, he could likewise decide to go, he could tip his uncertainty across into whatever freedom he desired. That was for him to decide.

As she lifted the top of her laptop and turned it on she heard the sound of Philippe upstairs, and a murmur of voices as he woke the driver Mahfouz. Perhaps Christopher would be hearing this also and wondering what was happening. She deleted the browser's cache and checked that the website hadn't left a cookie. She wiped out the singer Maya Yazbeck whose identity she had borrowed. Now she was no longer associated in any way with the message sent to the food writer's wife, the one called 'Thé Glacé' on the blogs, the small woman with pale hair who was also an artist, a well-known one. There would be no trace, not even a false one.

Now *I can go* was clear.

And yet it was not without anxiety that she went up the stairs towards the top floor of the truck drivers' house where Christopher was unlikely to be sleeping. She met Philippe and Mahfouz coming down from the floor below Christopher's, and signaled to them to be quiet, though she saw with a small heat of embarrassment that this was unnecessary given their manner, and was only the result of her own nerves. Mahfouz was respectfully carrying Philippe's small suitcase for him, and had his own backpack over one shoulder. They did not pause but went on down towards the truck garage at the back, where the freshly-painted red Mercedes saloon was parked. The doors of the rooms were all open except the one to the room she had used, where Christopher was no doubt waiting to find out what was happening.

How would she finish it, this *bizarre* episode of the food writer? In France there were houses with signs on their doors or gates that said, *Attention: chien bizarre!* As a doctor she had sometimes stood in the open door of an apartment and encountered the 'mad dog' languid with caresses in the arms of its owner. But was there not supposed to be a savage beast somewhere inside? As was the case with Abdul Yassou, who had worn his domestication so convincingly in the kisses he had bestowed on the cheeks and neck of his beloved Boutros, and on his adored wife?

But the food writer Christopher Hare she did not believe to be bizarre in this sense, though perhaps in others.

She felt the weight of the gun in her jacket pocket, something she did not want to feel again after this day – but would, in some fashion, if she had understood Philippe's kiss on her forehead. Her anxiety reached forward to turn the catch of the lock on the bedroom door. She would wait for Christopher to open it, and she would also wait to discover what she herself was going to say at that moment.

Or she could leave the door for Antun to unlock when he arrived later in the morning.

This was her anxiety. This choice.

From downstairs came the quiet mutter of the Mercedes in the garage. Now, yes, she had of course already decided, she would do it as she had envisaged. She took the gun from her pocket and slipped the safety catch. Then she unlocked the door and stepped back. She did not believe she would have to shoot the food writer, but she would have to convince him to wait until it was light, until they had been gone for some time, before he could answer his own question, 'I can go?'

But there was no sound from the room and the door did not open from the inside. Indeed, when she went carefully forward and listened at the door she could hear the man snoring gently.

Oh, he was a phenomenon, *bizarre* in some way even if not savage, this Christopher Hare. What had his life been like that he could be so content with his situation? With the consequences of his action and of what he now knew about its dangers?

She reversed the safety catch of the revolver and went quickly down the stairs, turning out the lights as she went. Her anxiety drained away, a sensation that was joyful at first. But soon after, there was an ache of grief in the very pit of her stomach as she put on her fine dark overcoat and took her bags to the garage, including the plastic one with the grey wig and her surgical gloves in it. Her grief came from the innocent sound of Christopher snoring, as if oblivious to what fate might now decide for him if he did not take his *I can go now* into his own hands.

She put her bags in the trunk of the red Mercedes and got into the back seat next to some boxes of brochures for Turkish leather shoes. The brochures smelled new, as did the paint on the car. She had gone most of a night without sleep but now felt if anything less weary than before, all her alert attention gathered as if checking the pulse of this critical moment.

She had left the door from the downstairs kitchen to the garage open, so that the food writer might at least be able to see that he could leave the house when he chose to. There was a small door in the side of the truck garage which led out to a concrete-paved courtyard with some plastic chairs and a rusty iron table, where the drivers and mechanics had left their cigarette butts and some tea-leaves thrown in arcs across the concrete. This small door he could unlock and open from the inside. The orderliness of her thoughts did not lessen the unexpected and, she thought, inappropriate ache of grief which was also an apprehension. When would Christopher wake up? Or what would wake him?

Neither Philippe nor Mahfouz spoke to her from the front

seat, nor did either of them turn to look at her. She sensed that Philippe had instructed Mahfouz in this behavior. The driver backed the car out of the garage carefully and without his usual flourishes, and got out to lower the steel roller door and secure it with a padlock.

Even without Mahfouz in the car, Philippe did not speak to her. He sat upright in the front passenger seat and gazed ahead as if there was something to look at. Perhaps he was looking at his thoughts. Unlike Mahfouz he had washed and shaved, and his grey hair was combed flat and moist above his ears. He had a faint aroma of Bay Rum, old fashioned – she knew it from her father when he came back into the house shining from his shave and barbering, with the newspaper in his hand.

To the last moment before the roller door closed she thought she might see the food writer appear hastily from the kitchen at the back of the garage. She could imagine him waving in a clumsy way, uncertain of what he was trying to communicate. But he did not appear, did not wave. As the car turned down the dark street away from the truck drivers' house, Philippe snapped his fingers once, in the air beside his left ear.

'*Khalas.*' Finished.

No, Philippe, she thought. It is not. For her, perhaps, something was only now beginning. And for the food writer, when he woke up from the innocence of his sleep, there would remain the question, *I can go now?*

With the headlights of the Mercedes now on they drove circumspectly by the lowest coast road through Cap-d'Ail to Monaco, because there was less surveillance than on La Provençale with the toll-booths. Still no one in the car spoke as they drove on the slow road through Villefranche, Beaulieu and Èze. These were innocent places whose season of entertainment and revenue was still some months distant, so the traffic of supply vehicles and of police was minimal.

The red Mercedes of the importer of Turkish shoes and cheap kitchenware drove carefully along the coast which was beginning to lighten with dawn, towards the establishments of the many clients who would wish to restore their inventories during the quiet season. This was a sober, normal business venture and they had made a good, early start.

It was that time of day when the horizon was lost at the place where the sea and the sky meet, an effect increased by the season, whose pale grey mists might have been either water or air, you could not tell the difference; and so the first pink light of dawn came without any strong sense that this was a new day beginning.

At the approach to Monaco, the traffic slowed to accommodate those descending from La Provençale, though there were not many. Even so, the passage through Monaco was congested, but Mahfouz remained patient and refrained from his usual tirades about shit as they drove slowly by the marina with its off-season rows of white, uninhabited yachts. Here, Philippe made a gesture towards the parking lot.

'*Huna*.'

There was a large container for rubbish and she put the bag with the grey wig and the surgical gloves into it. Philippe was smoking at the edge of the water, walking slowly up and down, an elegant old man stretching his legs, taking an interest in the luxurious boats. He was wearing a plain grey tweed Italian jacket with a dark pashmina scarf. A prosperous merchant with his driver, and an assistant or business partner perhaps – the tall dark woman, who seemed even a little bored and haughty, displeased at having made such an early start. Perhaps one day this businessman would like to have such a fine boat as one of these – but meanwhile there was work to be done, and a journey, clearly.

At that moment she had the sensation of stepping across an invisible threshold into an alternative world, the one that Philippe had already imagined as it would be seen by those passing casually, barely noticing and not remembering the red Mercedes and its passengers, who would in any case not interest them. Or if they did remember anything, it would be that the Mercedes was red, not a white taxi. Such arrangements were what Philippe did. She had observed this; he was like an artist or a film director in this capacity. *He saw what others would see.*

And soon she would take her key from the concierge at the apartment building in Geneva – yes, it was good to be back, thank you – and she would be in yet another world whose connection to the double shooting in Le Lapin Sauvage would be even more improbable.

Now, at last, was she beginning to be tired? These were not after all contesting realities, but all aspects of the single one. Even so, she had to make an effort to be where she was, in that moment. She could see that Philippe was looking closely at the surroundings. When he turned from the yachts and looked at her, she experienced the slight nod of his head like a shock, like the instant, early most mornings, when her cellphone alarm made the urgent, insistent sound of a song thrush, four notes the same, and she was awake.

There were oily streaks on the thick, dark, slowly heaving surface of the harbour below the edge of the marina, and when she dropped the revolver, an iridescent eddy dissipated quickly from the place where it had sunk.

In the car again, one word from Philippe, '*Yallah.*' Go.

And then Mahfouz began to sing – glancing sideways at Philippe as if for permission, drumming on the steering wheel – softly at first, and then, when no one told him to be quiet, with enjoyment and relief, because now at last they were about to be finished with this work.

Yallah yallah yallah!

'*Habibi Ya Eini – yallah ya Bassem*, you know it, Maya Yazbeck sang it, when I go to heaven I will fuck her.'

'My friend, everybody knows this song, and when they get

to heaven every man will be ahead of you.' Philippe patted the driver on his shoulder. 'But good luck, my friend.' To her, in the back seat, 'With respect, excuse us, Professor.'

Of course, Mahfouz was ignorant of the false identity she had now discarded.

Both men were singing and clapping as the red Mercedes ascended through the narrow streets of Monte Carlo towards Cap Martin, *Yallah yallah yallah. Habibi ya eini. Ya eini ya leili. Yam sahar eini. Bein hari wi leili!*

Love, oh my eyes
Oh my eyes, my nights
My eyes that can't sleep
By day or by night!

It was natural that they would feel this way, and she could also see that Philippe, with his usual skill, was indulging Mahfouz, because if the driver was happy he would pay less attention to what it was they had left behind them in the truck drivers' house. He would not dwell on the question of the food writer, assuming that the *chef de mission* and his clever Doctor would have taken care of that situation.

They came over Cap Martin above the large grey bay of Carnolès and Menton, and there was Italy at the far side of the bay, with the sombre sunrise lighting the rough cliffs and hills that rose inland, and the windows of houses and apartment buildings reflecting back the tints of morning. Then the men in the front seat stopped singing the Maya Yazbeck song, after how many times, perhaps because now they could see between the top of the cape and the distant, misty end of the bay the penultimate stage of their journey towards the conclusion of this game – away from 'the one left behind', she thought, imagining the road between Nice and Genoa as the track of a backgammon board, along which they were moving according to Philippe's strategy, and according to his compliance with the strategy of his former leader, al-Hakim, her own father's cousin, that George Habash, who had so often advocated 'the one left behind' as effective *tric trac*.

But also according to his compliance with her interpretation of that strategy.

With the border in front of them and the day beginning to produce the early walkers of little dogs on the Carnolès promenade, they were approaching the moment when 'the one left behind' would need to act. There was no longer any surveillance of consequence on the border but they took the uphill route through Garavan and left the territory of the French police past the tax-free liquor store on the Italian side, where some early customers were already drinking coffee and smoking on the little terrace by the shop, waiting for it to open. And then they crossed the hill and descended on the Italian side towards Ventimiglia.

Then, for the first time, Philippe permitted himself a few words. He remained gazing ahead with a calm upright posture, so that she had to lean forward to hear what he was saying in his factual, engineer's voice. In doing so she leaned into the scent of his Bay Rum and cigarette, her father's morning aroma. She would always regret her father's disapproval of her even as she treasured his pride in her professional accomplishments. Inside him, she knew, he had carried a shame ever since leaving Lydda, and the question, *What if we had stayed?*

'My friends,' said Philippe formally as if addressing colleagues for whom he had no particular feelings, 'now we are for the moment beyond the immediate surveillance of the French, though who knows whether there are others with a more urgent motivation.'

What if they had stayed? Her father's question sat to the side of her mind as she attended to what Philippe was saying. Mahfouz had again become tense, and began to interrupt Philippe, who stopped him with a hand on his arm.

'Yes, we are perhaps just out of sight of whoever may be looking for the woman who committed two murders last night and the driver of the white taxi that took her away. And we may be wondering about the complication that arose. But I want to say to you: *mabrouk,* my friends, we accomplished what we set out to do and now each of us knows what to do next. So that is the main thing.'

If her father's family had not fled in the weeks before *al-Nakba,* would the white-stone house still be there, in Lydda? Would they, rather, have joined that procession of people walking towards Barfiliya – the pale, hot image that was as real in her mind as if she had been there? Would her grandmother have survived that walk? Her mother, pregnant with her brother? How often she had rebuked herself for these stupid questions, for which there were no answers, because the only circumstance in which it was possible to live was the present one – and yet she knew that in some way they expressed her father's shame, which she had tried to redeem through her own actions, through her disobedience and subsequently her stupid risks, of which he had disapproved. Especially her going to Beirut with Boutros, to the apartment of that mad dog, her husband, which was certainly the cause of his grandson's death.

'And as for that complication,' Philippe continued, turning then just a little to look at Mahfouz whose neck had become tight with worry, 'our colleague the Doctor has taken care of that. So we will not speak about it again. Not among ourselves.' His hand on the driver's arm again. 'And not to any other person.'

Which was when her father had begun to go unshaven for days at a time, taking his coffee in pyjamas on the rooftop, leaving the newspaper unopened on the large table downstairs, smelling like an old man and not of Bay Rum and his daily ration of one Turkish cigarette.

'And now,' said Philippe as they crossed the river to

Ventimiglia, 'let us have a coffee together, since the Italians at least know how to do it.'

This was his joke, to break the moment of tension over the 'complication'. He gave the driver's arm a squeeze to be friendly but also to mark his instruction to remain silent.

That was where he died, her father, without warning, in his pyjamas, his coffee spilled across the little table at his side – on the roof of his house on Jebel Ashrafieh, in the very place her grandmother had once occupied with her rehearsed performances, facing west, towards what he had left behind over there, the Mar Jirjes to protect the house of his marriage, his necessity, his decision, his shame.

They had coffee and some slices of onion focaccia in weak, chilly sunshine outside a café by the market. The place was busy and loud with early shoppers and with porters and vendors. None of them had eaten substantially the night before, but it was Mahfouz who was hungriest – he ordered another portion and also a slice of frittata. The energy with which he ate and the effort it was costing him to remain silent about the food writer were equally apparent in his nervous gestures, his eyes sometimes downcast and at others flicking about, avoiding hers. He had the guilty expression of someone embarrassed by his hunger and his manners, and at the same time defiant in his sense of entitlement.

Philippe was watching him carefully, she saw; he was watching where this fissure in Mahfouz might open and release something they would all regret. And at a certain moment, turning as if to wipe his mouth on a paper napkin, the old man looked at her directly, and when he had her attention, gestured quickly with his eyebrows at the driver.

'*Mi piace l'italiano*,' he said softly, meaning, speak Italian. He gestured at the plate from which Mahfouz had just taken the last of his frittata. 'The food, the coffee, it's better.' His chin lifted the conversation in her direction.

'I, too, prefer Italian food,' she said, hearing a kind of

falseness in her voice. 'And you, Mahfouz?'

He was looking at her suspiciously, in case she was making fun of his appetite. 'I prefer Italian whores,' he said, in the French-sounding accent of Genoa.

'The food writer likewise,' she persisted, accepting the driver's coarse joke. 'Though as to the whores, he didn't tell me.' Then she built a short bridge for herself. 'But I learned something about his wife.'

She saw the driver's attention focus quickly – he put the remnant of his frittata down and waited, chewing slowly.

'The last message he wished to leave for his wife was, *food is love*.'

Then Mahfouz was calculating the parts of what she had just said. His eyes on her while he put the last piece of food in his mouth and chewed it.

This was a cunning and resourceful man who concealed his knowledge of the world behind his vocabulary of shit and whores. But she knew he had survived as a teenage guerrilla without mother or father in the camp at Bourj el-Barajneh under the Israeli air strikes, and when the *fedayeen* left Beirut in August of 1982 he had gone with them on the boats with a piece of shrapnel still in his back, first to Algiers and then by stages to Genoa, where he learned to fix and on occasion to steal the cars he then drove to the ferry at Malaga and to the operators of taxis in Morocco. She knew of the deep cavity under his right shoulder-blade where shrapnel had been removed, because she had looked at it when she saw he still felt pain these many years later, and she knew his deafness in one ear was one reason why his manner was sometimes aggressive or defiant.

But also, he had been where she had not. He had been born in west Beirut in the camp, he had been orphaned, he had fought, he had been wounded, he had endured the days of air strikes. And when he looked steadily at her with his eyes that were capable of seeing her dissemble, she also saw a certain careful scorn in his expression, because although he respected her work as a doctor for children, not to mention what she had shown she was capable of in the restaurant the night before, he also knew that she had not been born and brought up in a place like Bourj el-Barajneh and had not hidden underground waiting for the roof to collapse on her under the weight of the bombardment. And then there was the matter of the food writer, which he was forbidden to discuss, but which she could see he did not respect her for.

So when she said 'the last message', he was not permitted to interrogate her about the complete meaning of what she had said, but was expected to draw his own conclusion. She watched him thinking about it, knowing she was at least his equal in the challenge of her expression. And also because, in her heart, and in the grief that lingered in the pit of her stomach, she believed the matter had indeed been taken care of.

'*Food is love.*' Mahfouz spoke the phrase warily, as if searching for its code. 'This was the *last thing* he said?'

'It was his farewell message for his wife.' She held the convenient truth of this in her expression as Mahfouz looked at her, still with a certain disbelief. 'What do you make of that?' she asked him, leading his thoughts away from the question at the heart of his doubt.

And then, at last, he seemed to relax a little. He pushed his finger through the oil on his plate and sucked it. His eyes drifted to the young woman cutting focaccia slices on the marble bench at the front of the café.

Then he spoke quietly in Arabic, his voice reaching back into his throat for the sound and shape of the poetry.

If I am hungry
I will eat the flesh of my usurper.
Beware of my hunger
And of my anger.

She knew it, a poem of Mahmoud Darwish, 'Identity Card'. It was a poem that was always quoted, the children of the camps still learned it, forty years after it was written. When the woman cutting focaccia saw that Mahfouz was looking at her, she put a fist on her hip, challenging him, and he looked away, embarrassed.

'Let's go,' he said, returning to his Genoese Italian. But then, quietly, he added more lines from 'Identity Card'.

My palm is solid as rock
Scratching whoever touches it
And to me the most delicious food
Is olive oil and thyme.

'Yes,' he said. 'That would be true.' He wiped his finger on the oily plate again and licked it. 'If it comes to that.' And then again, 'Let's go.'

His manner was even a little surly, as if he felt he had been outwitted. Philippe was still sipping his coffee in a leisurely manner, so the driver's impatience was also impolite.

'And yours?' she asked Philippe, to smooth the moment.

In quiet Arabic also, despite his own instruction, Philippe recited some lines.

The conquerors have arrived
And the former conquerors have gone.
Difficult to remember my face
In the mirrors . . .

'That is also Darwish,' he said. 'But who can have a favourite star in such a firmament? And the favourite food? The food of love?' He lifted the small cross on its chain around his neck, and kissed it. 'What one has just eaten, thank God.'

Then they were both looking at her. She felt the moment

as a farewell, so that her throat swelled against what she tried to say.

'At the funeral of Darwish in Ramallah the streets were hung with banners, with his image on them and one word: Farewell. For me it was as though everything he ever wrote was in that word. Always that leave-taking, one exile after another.'

She refrained from telling them that her favourite food was not Arab or Italian, but would always be Argentinian, the rich *joues de boeuf* that she and Abdul Yassou would eat at Le Baratin, in that false present from which she had now gone forward.

She knew that her face was hard with the effort of controlling her emotions, but even so the driver smiled at her. His teeth were very bad and usually he concealed them behind his hand, but now he displayed them as if to say, what have we to hide?

'Yes,' said Mafouz. 'Farewell. '*Ma'a as-salaama.*'

Then he stood and walked towards where the car was parked, two or three streets away from the bustle of the market.

Philippe sat in silence for a moment before lifting his hand for the bill. He was watching the driver disappear without fuss in the crowd of people arriving at the market. They were becoming more numerous now, and there were some municipal police and *carabinieri* also beginning to appear in the street. They were known to check the papers of Arabs and blacks, or those who resembled them, or those who looked away too quickly.

Soon the two of them would follow Mahfouz to the car and then, before long, they would arrive by the autostrada at Genoa.

'He has the instinct of a great thief,' said Philippe. 'He will not be seen and therefore he will not be caught. Never.' He looked at her and smiled, and she felt his affection and approval warm her face in a blush. 'But you, Doctor – you survived his investigation I think. Thank you. This is very hard to do, as I know from experience. As do others.'

Then, after finding the money for their breakfast, he looked at his watch, and then at her, tapping the face of the watch. She at once knew what he was doing. Piece by piece, move by move, along the route, through the time it would take, and always leaving behind the only place from which to go forward, he was approaching the end of the game.

'Yes,' he said. 'Doctor Habash. There is the piece left behind. Always, the piece left behind.' He took her arm, and they walked back towards the car, the prosperous-looking elderly man in his fine Italian coat with the striking woman who might have been his wife or perhaps his mistress of many years.

She knew that Philippe was directing her in a performance for the eyes of others. The handsome *carabiniere* officer looked at her with manly approval, and she saw that he was impressed by the manner in which *la signora* ignored him, so that as she passed he touched his fingers to his cap with regret and admiration.

CHAPTER 10

Nana Gobbo's superannuated border collie would sit imploringly outside the glass door to the verandah with a foam-dripping twig in his mouth. Beyond him was the river that ran down to the wide bay, with the untidy lines of white breakers at the bar, through which Uncle Antonio used to angle his battered Parkercraft at speed. Sometimes he would appear next to the imploring dog on the outside of the glass door, holding up a wriggling crayfish by the back of its shell. Both he and the dog had similar expressions of helpless longing on their faces, and both were bearing gifts with which to win entry to Nana Gobbo's house. Both usually got in, but they had to work hard for it.

It was Uncle Antonio who taught him how to clean and fillet fish and how to make a fish stock with the heads and bones, which you could always eat as a soup if you couldn't be bothered taking the thing any further. Uncle Antonio drank too much and it was the drink that one day caused him to miscalculate his speed run at the white water of the bar beyond the rivermouth, so that his old Parkercraft flipped and he washed up halfway down the beach hours later at low tide.

Christopher got the news from the cousin who'd pinned him on his back in the scratchy grass up in the orchard. She was the one who kept in touch, with short humorous letters that always ended 'Hope you are keeping well'. In this letter she'd written, 'Piss-head Antonio finally chugged the big one.'

He woke from a dream of a wide expanse of water, and the memory of the imploring dog and uncle was almost a part of the dream, but not quite – it followed as he woke with a stripe of sunlight across his face, having just been flying low in his own body across sea that was at once the ruffled blue of the bay out from Tolaga and the milky blue of the gulf off Chiavari. The boats that were crossing the gulf were like the little squidders that came back across Tigullio to Chiavari in the pink morning, and they were also like Uncle Antonio's cray boat. He flew low past their wakes with his mouth open and the wide expanse of the blue space funnelling into him. He flew across the watery space, consuming it, and felt a wake spreading out behind him, but not on the surface of what he was crossing and swallowing into his weightless body, but rather a kind of void, empty and tranquil.

And then, as he woke with a dry mouth and a stab of discomfort from the light in his eyes, came the memory of the dog with its drooled twig, and next, of optimistic Uncle Antonio with his struggling crayfish. They were on the outside looking in. The glass door of the verandah was somehow where the dream and the memory met.

So, it was morning. He'd slept without expecting to. There was a damp patch on the pillow where he'd dribbled a little; his sleep must have been deep. He was dying for a piss, and desperate for water. There was half a bottle of mineral water on a table at the end of the bed, and a towel over a chair. He drank from the bottle, imagining the woman's sarcastic lips gripping it. The towel retained a faint trace of her perfume, and he hung it over his shoulder and took it to the door. There he banged hard with the flat of his hand on the grubby paint and shouted.

'Hello! *Il y a quelqu'un*?'

Suddenly the panicky thought that they might have gone already and he hadn't heard them. The little bag in the woman doctor's hand, her grand overcoat. He banged again, and then began to rattle the door by its handle. And then he just turned it, and the door opened towards him.

Why hadn't he thought of doing that first? He went quickly across the landing, feeling the sheepish grin on his face as if he'd been watching himself make the assumption that he'd still be locked in. But why wouldn't he assume that? He pissed with enormous relief into the squat toilet, which he saw had been thoroughly cleaned, and then threw water over his face and head at the basin, which was also clean. Then he dried himself with the towel scented by Dr. Hawwa Habash.

Where was she?

He knew the feeling that now began to invade his guts – an apprehensive nausea that made his palms and his top lip sweat. He pushed it away with a deep breath and focused on where he was.

The other door to the landing was open, and he could see the green armchairs and the table in the dim interior of the room where he'd first been locked up. He went in and opened the window and the shutters, revealing the eastern walls of buildings lit by the early morning sun, and the hillsides north-west of the city standing out against strong shadows. So he had some idea of where he was, facing roughly north-west.

He didn't feel any need to hurry. It seemed clear enough now that the woman and whoever else had been in the house had already left – the driver with the thick, sweating neck and the quiet elderly man who had appeared from time to time – but he checked every room on the floor below to be sure. The doors to the rooms were open as if to make his investigation both easy and unnecessary: two bedrooms and a smaller, dirtier lavatory than upstairs. The whole place smelled grubby, of cigarettes and old cooking, and the bedding and towels seemed hastily abandoned, thrown aside as if expecting a cleaning service. But there was no sign of any kind of individual use, no clothes or personal belongings. The squirms of nausea continued, but he moved on as if to keep ahead of the panic that awaited his surrender.

On the ground floor was a larger room with a table and chairs, a fridge, and a dirty stove. Some used glasses and coffee cups had been left in the sink; a rubbish bin spilled over with oily paper food wrappings and chicken bones. There was a pot on the stove: he lifted its lid and found the cold remains of the scorched chickpeas he remembered smelling the night before. A short passage led to a street door, which was locked.

He hesitated for a moment at the locked door with his trembling hand on the latch and then went back to the kitchen room. He remembered having originally come in through what smelled like a garage. Maybe that would be a less conspicuous way to leave.

But he knew he was also hesitating and delaying something – 'dithering' was Miss Pepper's word. It had always made her top lip lift off her teeth.

Because it was true: he felt shakily apprehensive at the thought of going out. As the woman had been at pains to tell him, he was now carrying a bag of dangerous shit. He had to think this through. What if the house was being watched? And by whom?

But there was another, vaguer question, which was more difficult. *Why* was he leaving? What *for*?

And what was all that about having to send a message to TG? '*Food is love.*' Along with his memory of the blissful look on her face when she put the first forkful of *joues de boeuf* in her mouth at Le Baratin, he'd always remember her saying, 'What is it, Christopher?' when Luigi put the *Cappon Magro* in front of her at Boccadasse and he burst into tears. *What is it?* It was love, Pepper, crazy love. The words he'd wanted to say had swelled up in his throat and he couldn't get them out. He'd felt like a complete fuckwit, seeing her lovely neat head tipped a little to the side like a bird, that row of white nippy teeth just showing in what was probably a smile but you couldn't ever be sure.

'Don't be a dolt, Christopher.'

Yes, but also he'd seen what it had cost her to hold something back that night, that tightness in her face, her stare that *dared* him to get it wrong, when he'd finally blurted out the words, 'Will you marry me?'

At the Santa Chiara in Boccadasse, Luigi thought she was hot, but Luisa had asked, 'Are you sure, *Chris-tuh-fuh*?'

Yes, he was.

But now he was dithering, trying to come to terms with the dumb feeling of disappointment and abandonment that had moved up on him as he explored the empty rooms. What had been the point of his crazy exploit? Had he really expected that the rush of his first impulse, when he'd run past the maître d' with his 'No! No!' or 'Go! Go!' expression, would keep pushing him forward?

The answer was, he hadn't known what to expect. Look, here he was, wandering around, opening cupboards and looking into abandoned rooms, for fuck's sake. The truth was, he couldn't explain what he'd done or why he'd done it. '*Why did you do it!*' The rage of the tall, bony woman that made the question into a curse, that left a fleck of froth on her lip. To escape the present he was stuck in, was what he'd said. She'd seemed to understand what he meant. Maybe she'd understood it better than he had. But what was next, now that he was free, now that he was in the place from which he could move forward?

He remembered her expression as she left the room he'd fallen asleep in with one nostril pressed to the faint trace of her aroma. Her disdainful face was closed, yes, but closed *against* something. She was ready to go, with her bag and her large Italian coat, but there had been some kind of goodbye behind her shut face, a message. One she'd decided to keep to herself, unlike his absurd *food is love* spilled out there shamelessly. What might she have wanted to say? 'Good luck?' With what – his future? 'Run for your life?' Yes, the bag was full of danger, but what in the end did that have to do with him?

Or: *Why don't you come with us?*

He pushed his nausea down with a groan. Of course that's what he'd begun to hope for. That he might amount to something else, working with her, with the children.

And then there was the matter of the maître d'. If he'd understood Doctor Habash correctly, the guy was part of the whole thing. He was one of *them*. And he'd be coming around to this house, or so she'd insisted. So why had they left without him, the hairy fucking maître d', one of the *gang*?

Now he was getting really pissed off. He walloped a cupboard with the flat of his hand and a paper bag of dried chickpeas fell out and spilled across the floor. Fucking mess! It was a total fucking mess, the whole situation. He didn't get it.

On the other side of the kitchen room, through a door with a pair of filthy overalls hanging on a hook, was a small, cluttered pantry or passage. Off the passage was another open door, from which came a stink of diesel and also something like the acrid chemical smell he'd noticed the night before. He found the light switch and under bright industrial lamps saw a large empty garage with an oil-stained floor, a workbench cluttered with tools, a block-and-tackle on a gantry mounted under the high roof, a couple of heavy-duty wheeled jacks, and what looked like a lube pit covered with steel plates. He investigated a wheelie bin. It was the source of the chemical smell, stuffed with sheets of masking paper and tape sprayed with red paint.

All this seemed to confirm was that they'd gone. Buggered off. They'd been preparing to go the whole time the doctor sat with him in the upstairs room trying to get information from him, but also trying to explain something to him. But never really letting him in on what they were doing. Well, why would she? He was her 'problem'. Again, he had the humiliating sensation of observing his own absurdity – his pangs of disappointment and anger at being excluded from their plans, the car-painting, the getaway schemes. All his rage slumped into the disappointment. Why couldn't he have gone with them?

'For fuck's sake, get a grip,' he said aloud, as he tried the small door in the side of the garage. It was locked, but he found the catch and unfastened it. That lurch of apprehension again in his guts. A space opened out and he peered into it. There was an empty concrete yard with a few battered chairs arranged around a table, against a white, plastered wall. The shabby courtyard was filled with early morning sunshine and looked inviting after the smelly interior of the house, but he closed and relocked the door and went back to the kitchen.

There, he stood with his eyes shut and his hands pressed flat on the table. He made himself breathe deeply, and relax. That fluttering in his chest, the nausea, and a burning sensation like dyspepsia in his stomach where, not so long ago, there'd been a pleasant calmness. What had that been about? The sense of leaving behind a kind of shop-window dummy propped up in the restaurant window – the sense of having escaped from himself.

Something similar had happened when he arrived in Chiavari the first time, with his paltry scraps of Italian and a phone number for some kind of cousin. Rain and wind were blasting in from the sea, and grey waves were surging across the breakwater along the beach. *Mi chiamo Christopher*, he'd practiced even though he no longer felt like the Christopher who'd assisted Uncle Antonio across the back yard to the shade awning, after his famous farewell lunch at Nana Gobbo's place in Tolaga Bay.

'Mi chiamo Christopher,' he said aloud, now, and began

to cry without restraint in the kitchen of the empty house with its unnervingly deserted feel and its stink of car paint. 'È un piacere conoscerla.' *I am very happy to know you.* His own deserted feel, like the house. A sordid emptiness. He let the grief take over and bellowed, feeling the snot running over his lip, down his chin.

He'd gone with the 'cousin', an elegant middle-aged woman who'd dressed with care to welcome him in a fine coat with a silk scarf, to a house up in the hills behind Chiavari. There, with more 'cousins', he ate a winter soup of veal-stuffed cabbage parcels in clear veal stock, chestnut gnocchi with pesto, potatoes and pumpkin, roast rabbits with mushrooms and olives, and pandolce fruit cake with sweet, sticky wine. At each course he was toasted, until his face began to ache with smiling. Then they all drank a few rounds of grappa and began to sing. It was familiar, just like the get-togethers and singalongs at Nana Gobbo's place back at the Bay. He'd sung his Dean Martin standard to loud applause.

Then he'd slept in a comfortable double bed which had been warmed with hot water bottles and whose pillows had been sprinkled with lavender oil, and only when he tried to go out for a tipsy pee during the night and got lost in the house did he realise that his 'cousin' and her husband had given him their bed and were sleeping on a fold-out couch in the room where they'd all had dinner. In the morning they sent him off with a handwritten list of places to go and eat in all the way back along the coast from Bocca di Magra to Genoa.

His secret Bible. Pure gold.

But now it was time to move on again. His fit of weeping had passed and, as usual, he looked back at it and saw it for what it was, just something he did. Self-pity, TG used to call it, but she didn't know about the feelings of loss that his occasional floods of tears opened him up to.

And as usual, when he'd finished, he felt a teary kind of

relief. He blew his crybaby nose on a paper towel from a roll by the stove. There was a blackened *imbriki* coffee-pot on one of the gas rings, and a paper bag of ground coffee on the bench next to the stove. He sniffed the coffee – a strong smell of cardamom. It reminded him of Christopher Hare and Mary Pepper's *fabulously* successful *1,001 Nights* book. So he dumped the old grounds from the pot into the sink and filled it with fresh water. Why not?

If he was honest with himself, he could probably identify the moment when TG began to leave. It was that night in Wadi Rum. At the end of the *mansaf* they drank strong, pale, bitter coffee poured from a beaky pot with cardamom twigs stuffed in its spout. A little cup for yourself, another for the host, a third for Allah, was what he'd understood. Then you waggled the empty cup to indicate you'd had enough, and put it upside-down on the tray. He was watching Miss Pepper – she'd gone out of the tent and then come back in. When she came back in he saw that she'd retreated to the carefully polite shell from which she usually emerged in a rage. But not this time. Back at the hotel in Amman she simply showered and then got into bed with her back to him.

'Goodnight, Christopher,' she'd said. 'That was interesting, wasn't it.'

He'd known better than to touch her. And then, later, there was the moment with the proof-sheets. TG's photograph of the *mansaf* with all the hands reaching in.

'Fuck you Christopher, you're so wet. *You* decide. Why don't you choose the whole lot all by your fucking self.'

He didn't know what she was on about. Or he did, but why couldn't they go on making the most of what they had? He felt her pulling away.

Cause if you liked it then you should have put a ring on it, sang Beyoncé, TG singing along, her music thing, and he wanted to say, *but I did, Pepper, look!* Her pale, slender finger with the turned-up tip, the shiny nail, the thin gold band. By then they were almost finished. And often she sang it, or the other songs, with her iPod on, so all he could hear was her half-pie listening-singing voice, that faraway look in her eyes.

But we did. Put a ring on it. *We* did.

When the *imbriki* boiled on the stove he took it off and spooned in some of the cardamom-scented coffee grounds. Then he left it to settle.

He was getting a grip. Maybe he'd do some cooking again. Go back to London and tell Bob to stick his magazine up his arse. Mind you, that would be a waste of time. Bob had already told him to stick it up his own.

He was beginning to cheer up.

Still, he couldn't let go of that feeling he'd been dumped. Which had something to do with the maître d', whose look of panic he now remembered vividly. And who, as Hawwa Habash had said, *being unreliable, was a great danger to them at this time. And therefore.*

Maybe he was going to find out soon.

An absurd little surge of hope. He knew it was absurd – but maybe the maître d' would be his link to the future that had sped off before dawn in the red-painted white taxi.

The smell of the freshly brewed, cardamom-infused coffee was indescribably enticing. He washed out a glass and gave the coffee a cautious stir with the handle of a spoon. Then he remembered what he'd seen them do in street-front coffee shops in places like Damascus and Beirut, tapping the side of the pot with a spoon to make the grounds settle. He drummed out a little rhythm on the side of the *imbriki* – shave-and-a-haircut, Bay-Rum! – and then carefully poured himself a glass of the fragrant brew.

Going back to cooking maybe wasn't such a bad idea. A sudden memory made him snicker: they'd been relaunching the smash hit Ligurian book on TV, as a series, and he was demonstrating how to make a thin *focaccia* dough –

thinner and thinner, a wonderful elastic sheet that he held up triumphantly, then tripped and accidentally draped it over his own face. So what was he meant to do? He bit a hole out for his mouth, tore two more for his eyes, and intoned, 'Don't try this at home.' He thought the footage was hilarious. But TG wasn't laughing and the producer just said, 'Christopher, we're not doing comedy.'

Why not?

On to the octopus tartlets. No, he shouldn't have done the *Aliens* impersonation and then chucked the thing across the set. Or set fire to the tablecloth with the grilled figs *fiammeggiati*.

Did he have any idea how much this studio time was costing? No, he didn't, and he didn't give a fuck either. Why couldn't they lighten up?

Why couldn't he *grow* up, was TG's response to that.

'Jesus Christ, Chris-to-pher, why don't you just run around the place with a great big sign with "Look at me, Mum!" written on it?'

Oh yes, she knew how to hurt him. So they did the figs again, once the floor manager had been persuaded to come back, and closed with the bit where Mary Pepper and Christopher Hare clink glasses, turn to the camera, and say *buon appetito*!

'I liked the other versions better. This one's boring.'

'You would, Christopher. But you were just showing off, really. Don't you ever know when to stop?'

Apparently it wasn't funny anymore. But it used to be. And fun. And no, he didn't know when to stop, or why he should.

His hand was trembling a little as he lifted the hot glass of cardamom-scented coffee to his also trembling lips. It wasn't sadness he was feeling, more a kind of anticipation, because here he was: he'd moved on from TG and now he'd also moved on from the Christopher Hare propped up in the window of Le Lapin Sauvage, and, even further back, from the stupid Rosenstein he'd hidden behind years ago. He was empty, a bit of a mess, but ready for the next thing, whatever it was. He should just get the hell out of there as fast as possible and think the future through somewhere else, like back in London. Absolutely what he should do. Abort the trip. Go.

But the thin, astringent coffee bit his taste buds fiercely and filled his nose with its aromatic tang, so that he uttered a loud 'Ah!' of satisfaction and smacked his lips, and lingered. Yes, to be going forward, that was the thing. Perhaps, after all, there might be something Christopher Hare could do in the world that the tall, intense doctor with the exhausted, alert eyes and the strong hands had given him a glimpse of. A world he'd only ever seen inside a showcase Bedouin tent in Wadi Rum, or in Ducasse's dreadful Tamaris joint in Beirut. Or in that garden place in Damascus where TG plucked a small grilled object from a tray, popped it in her mouth and then realised it was an entire tiny bird, a sparrow or something. Spat it across the table. No-shit Pepper.

Maybe there was a way he could help with those kids the doctor worked with. She'd even seemed to hint that he might be useful, in some way.

His hands were still trembling a little so he put the glass of coffee down on the dirty table and did half a dozen toe-touches (but not quite) and side-stretches. Rolled his head around on his neck. Those weird grinding sounds again.

He topped up his glass of coffee and walked quickly, decisively, crunching the spilled chickpeas underfoot, to the garage and the little door to the yard outside. Decisiveness, that was the thing. As well as teaching him how to clean and fillet fish, Uncle Antonio had taught him how to chop the heads off Nana Gobbo's young roosters, before they got too big. You had to be decisive. Hold them upside down by the feet until they went quiet, then grip their wings behind their backs, neck over the block, whack! If you hesitated, the thing would always be a disaster with flapping and hoarse shrieks. Moving decisively always helped him to make decisions. He stooped quickly through the door and out into the bright sunlight of the yard.

The light was low and glaring from the concrete and from the white-painted wall at the back. Almost blinded, he hesitated and then stepped across to one of the plastic chairs by the table. He sat down, shading his eyes. He could smell the cigarettes that had been ground out on the concrete around the table. Finish the coffee first. Then he would decide what was next.

He was awake to the day, at last, fully out in it. He remembered Dr Habash's comment about what was wrong with thinking. The box was off. The rooster box.

'Cock-a-doodle-doo.' He sipped the bitter coffee.

I can go now?

Inside the house, the front door slammed. He recognised the voice of the maître d', calling out. The voice called out again, faintly, and then again, from the upper floors. A door slammed violently, up there, and the man shouted something angrily, in the angry language. And again.

He sat there. He could feel the heat from the sun reflected on his back from the white plastered wall behind him. He knew his shirt was hanging out and he looked a complete mess. God, he was so hungry and thirsty. It was an old game of torment, but he couldn't resist – he pictured a tall cold glass of beer, a sharp Czech pilsner, and a simple sauerkraut and bratwurst roll, the cheap sort you got on German railway station platforms. His mouth flooded with saliva, but the sigh he heaved only drew in the diesel tainted air of the courtyard.

When the maître d' came through the garage door in his swift, sliding way, as if negotiating the spaces between tables, and saw Christopher sitting there against the white, sunlit wall, the man's expression went instantly from rage to the kind of insincere warmth the food writer had come to know so well. He looked at Christopher with the incurious courtesy of his profession. He might have been sizing up what kind of guest he was dealing with. Then his expression shifted ever so slightly; he ducked his head, and a faint smile denoting cautious respect lifted the corners of his moustache. He might have been thinking that this was a better-than-average window-table diner. We can seat him with a view of the street. He's alone, and so he's serious in some way. He hasn't dressed for an occasion, and so he's confident. He's looking at the window table without making anything of it – well, then, he can have it. He's definitely not trouble. Not even tonight.

Christopher knew what was going to happen when he saw the gun in the maître d's hand. But he couldn't help himself.

'No,' he murmured, 'you don't have to. I've decided.'

'Assalaam Alaikum,' said the maître d', with grave, professional charm. 'Laila sa'eda wa ahlaam ladida. Good night and sweet dreams.' He added the English as if to be courteous to his guest.

The look of smiling incredulity on the food writer's face stayed there while the black hole in his forehead welled with blood, which ran in a straight line past his nose and down into his open mouth. Then, for a moment he seemed to taste it, with a quick, spasmodic smacking of his lips, before falling slowly sideways, away from the mess he'd made on the white wall behind him.

NOTES

Much of the information in this novel – places, recipes, events such as those in Amman, Jordan in 1969–70 – derives from my experience and I am responsible for the accuracy (or not) with which I've incorporated it in this fiction. For other factual material, I am indebted to several accounts of which the following are the most important:

Helena Cobban, *The Making of Modern Lebanon*. London: Hutchinson & Co. Ltd., 1985.

Kamal Dib, *Warlords and Merchants: The Lebanese Business and Political Establishment*. Reading: Ithaca Press/Garnet Publishing Limited, 2004.

Robert Fisk, *Pity the Nation: The Abduction of Lebanon*. New York: Thunder's Mouth Press/ Nation Books, 2002.

Sandra Mackey, *Lebanon: A House Divided*. New York: W.W. Norton & Company, Inc., 2006.

Julie Peteet, *Landscape of Hope and Despair: Palestinian Refugee Camps*. Philadelphia: University of Pensylvania Press, 2005.

I am indebted to the scrupulously maintained websites of the Palestinian Refugee ResearchNet (PRRN) and the on-line databases of UNRWA (The United Nations Relief and Works Agency for Palestine Refugees in the Near East).

I recommend Lucio Galletto and David Dale's mouthwatering book, *Lucio's Ligurian Kitchen*. Crows Nest, NSW: Allen & Unwin, 2008. Grateful thanks to my son Penn, a brilliant chef, for reading an early draft and trying out recipes with me.

Grateful thanks also to my wife Donna Malane and old friend Russell Haley for their invaluable comments.

This book was written with the generous assistance of the University of Auckland/Creative New Zealand Michael King Writer's Residency in 2009.

I acknowledge my old friend and colleague Fawwaz Tuqan, who introduced me to Palestinian poets back in 1969, in particular the late Mahmoud Darwish, whose last reading filled a football stadium with 25,000 people in Beirut the year before his death in 2008.